# THE RIGHT CHOICE

*A Louisiana Love Book 1*

## DANYELLE SCROGGINS

PUBLISHING

ALSO BY DANYELLE SCROGGINS

Where the Booth, Jackson, and Kimbrel Family

Began...

A Louisiana Christmas Books 1 & 2

Love Me Again

Never Looking Back

Published by: Divinely Sown Publishing

The Right Choice

*A Louisiana Love Book 1*

Copyright © 2020 by Danyelle Scroggins

A LOUISIANA LOVE BOOK 1

First Edition paperback

10 9 8 7 6 5 4 3 2 1

Printed in the United States of America

Book Cover Design by Danyelle Scroggins

Cover Model: SHAWNA and MARLON CHOYCE

Exclusive discounts are available for office quantity purchases. For details, contact the publisher at the address above.

Printed in the United States of America

*To my God-son, Marlon, and his beautiful wife Shawna. I am so extra proud of you and I know you were his RIGHT CHOICE.*
*Love you both forever and always,*
*G-Mom Danyelle*

*"Loving kindness and truth have met together; Righteousness and peace have kissed each other."*

*Psalm 85:10*

# THE RIGHT CHOICE PROLOGUE

*January 26th, Grand Cane, Louisiana.* Jasmine sat on the balcony of her recently married brother's home and cried. She had no desire to be bothered or deal with anyone. All she wanted was to be left alone. It had been exactly three weeks since she left California pledging to never return to the city, nor to Vance.

She'd seen all she needed to see. And no one, not even her father—who had tried twice since her return—could convince her of anything different. Vance was no good, and not worth her time.

The only bad thing…their families were tied together forever, and there was nothing she could do about it. Uncle James was married to Vance's mother. Her older brother, Kane, was eager to plan the wedding of a lifetime to Vance's sister, Veronica, especially, after all the drama they had endured.

It would be too selfish to allow what transpired

between her and Vance to alter her feelings towards Valerie and Veronica. And it would be childish to walk around like they'd done something to her, when they had done nothing at all. So the best resolution was to stay hidden at J.J. and Jade's house, and pretend like no one existed except her and them.

Jasmine was beginning to think her father was right after all. No woman should move in with a man who hadn't married them, or play wife to a man who wasn't her husband.

For months, she'd believed that Vance loved her.

She cleaned, cooked, washed, and did everything a woman should do for a man except sex. At least she was smart enough to hold on to something until after they were married. But that still didn't help her hurting heart.

Now it was time to think about Jasmine.

Not Vance.

Not her father's business.

But Jasmine.

As soon as she could muster enough strength to talk about what happened and to answer the questions from her family, she would come out of hiding and face the music. Until then, she would cry behind the pain that came from the wrong voice and choice.

At least, until she was all cried out.

# CHAPTER 1

**D**ecember 29, California. Jasmine sat on a huge fluffy pillow in the corner of Vance's two-bedroom apartment. It had been quite the task convincing her family that their living together in California was best for them. But for some, it still hadn't worked. No one saw the move coming, and the surprise of it all provoked some heated conversations.

For Jasmine, some days the conversations still hurt. And today was one of those days. Sure, they had a valid argument. She'd fallen in love really quick with Vance. But what wasn't to love about him? He was charming, smart, loyal, and he was a Christian. Not in words only, he truly had a heart for God. And if she was right, he loved her.

Jasmine rose from the plush sofa and walked to the huge window overlooking the pool. With her shoulder pressed against the wall, she gazed at what appeared to be a happy family enjoying their day. Sort of how her family was the day after Christmas for Kane's birthday. All smiles until she and Vance made their big announcement.

Jasmine sighed. *I'm here now.* California was nothing like she thought it would be, but hanging out with Vance in his collegiate atmosphere was fun. Even his friends embraced her. The only thing she couldn't get used to— the groupies. The girls who hung around athletes praying to land a husband before they went into the league. Here, they ran in cliques, dressed in skimpy clothes, and were relentless when they found their target. They couldn't care less if the target had a woman at his side. To them— she was replaceable.

Thank God for Vance's no-disrespect clause. Only God knew whether it was for their good or hers. The first time Jasmine saw how disrespectful they were, she vowed to lay claws if they ever tried her. Instead, Vance blocked her own mode of act-right, like he was a line-backer protecting her, the quarterback. He demanded their respect, but then again was she still worth respect-ing? She'd gone against the grain of everything her parents taught.

Jasmine sighed and shifted her weight to her other leg. Word for word, over and over, she rehearsed their last conversation like the lyrics to a bad song.

*"You mean to tell me that my boys have more respect for marrying the woman first before they live together. And my*

*girl is running off to live with a fiancé like that's perfectly fine?" Jasper Sr. yelled like he was losing it.*

*"Dad, I'm not Jasper or Kane and I'm grown!" she yelled back.*

*"You might be grown, but you're making a childish decision. I'd prefer he marry you first and then y'all go wherever y'all want to go. Heck, you can go live in the woods of Cambodia if you want. But at least you'd be married and God can bless you."*

*"Dad, we are grown, and Vance and I have enough self-control to live together and not do the things married people do. And even if we did, Dad, we are two grown consenting adults who have a right to make their own decisions."*

*"If you were, we wouldn't be having this conversation. I believe I'm talking to a child who is out of her mind. You're going to leave your job, home, and everything you've built to go live in an overpriced two-bedroom get-up until y'all decide to get married. Absolutely ridiculous!"*

*"Jasper, enough! You two have been going back and forwards for the last five minutes, and I've listened to you both and I'm sick of it. We have done our part, Jasper. We have raised these children in the way they should go, and at some point, we have to give them room to make their own choices." Jessica pulled a crying Jasmine into her arms.*

*"Jessica, she's making a dumb mistake, baby," Jasper ranted.*

*"Dad, it's my dumb mistake to make, and maybe I'm more like you than J.J. and Kane," Jasmine countered.*

*"I've never hit you, Jasmine Booth, but you'd better be quiet right now before I—"*

*"Before you what, Jasper?" Jessica asked. "You'd better shut this down and now before you both make me mad. And you both know, you don't want that. Now, Jasmine is old enough to make her own decisions, and although we may not like them, they are hers to make. And Jasmine, no matter how crazy your dad is being, you will never disrespect your father in any way. Do you understand me?"*

*"Yes ma'am," Jasmine whined.*

*"If you and Vance have decided to make this type of move, you do know you are making it without our blessing but with us praying. We have witnessed many men use the cow up and then decide they don't want her. That's all we are saying. But this is the life and body God gave you. If you make the choice to abuse it, that's you. You alone will have to live and deal with the choices you make. But you will still be our daughter, and we will love you no less. Now go wash your face and go home to pack."*

"I do love you both." The last thing Jasmine said to her parents' before leaving. Almost hating she'd ever came. She knew they were disappointed, and now she was the cause of them being angry with one another. Her mother's eyes were the proof that Dad was in for a tongue-lashing like never before. And usually, it was her stance to protect her daddy from her fire breathing, no-nonsense, mother. But not that day.

Jasmine blew out another deep breath.

She hated to even think of her parents arguing, especially when the subject of their disagreement was her. She'd prefer it be one of her brothers or even Jade. No matter what, she wasn't changing her mind. What if she stayed and lost the best thing that could have ever happened to her? *Vance needs me, and I need him.*

Jasmine began to cry. "Lord, they don't know I've been suffering in silence," she mumbled through sniffles. "I went to work everyday, almost killing myself trying to prove I earned my job based upon work ethic and not my family ties."

She pulled a tissue from the coffee table, blew her nose, and closed her eyes laying her head in her hands.

Jasmine hated the stigma of being the Booth princess. She hated feeling like others thought her job was given instead of earned. She wanted others to see her as a mastered leveled businesswoman who made good decisions and wise choices concerning job, life, and her future. *A boss lady.*

But somehow the stench of being the Booths' princess and Vance's lady, was now overshadowing everything.

Jasmine turned away from the window and jumped.

"Vance, you startled me. When did you come in?"

"A few seconds ago. I kind of felt like I would scare you but I didn't want to interrupt your thoughts. Are you okay, Jasmine?"

"Yes, just thinking."

"About the last conversation you had with your parents again?"

"Yeah, sort of. Well, yeah."

"Do you want to go back to Louisiana?"

"And leave you?"

"Yes, that would definitely mean you'd be leaving me. But I know you've been troubled by how things went. I don't want to be the bad blood between you and your parents and truth is, I understand them perfectly."

"Vance, I know but it's not you. I needed to grow up and this was a grown-up move." Jasmine made air quotations. "No one except Mom, Jade, and Veronica know we sleep in separate rooms, and that we are keeping things holy. But, I'm not concerned. I'm staying right here until you go to training camp like we planned."

"Well, we could go ahead and get married."

"Vance, we are fine just like we are. It hurts that I've let them down, but as long as God knows, He's all that matters."

"Okay, boss-lady, I'm riding with you, but at the same time, I'm praying for us."

"That's all I can ask of you. I love you, Vance."

"I love you, Jasmine Booth. The future Mrs. V. Kimbrel."

"Sounds good to me."

# CHAPTER 2

Veronica moved around her loft apartment cleaning and dusting off shelves. It had been non-stop since the Christmas in The Field event. Her mother and future brother-in-love, J.J., were both married, and Jasmine, her future sister-in-love, was now living in California with her brother.

Everything was peaceful except the latter, which had been a battle in itself. No one, not even her, understood why they would move together before they married. And although she and Kane were against it, neither of them inserted their opinion.

Veronica wasn't sure of his reasoning. But she knew all too well the hurricanes that brewed when siblings told siblings what they should or shouldn't do. Her mom, Valerie, and her sister, Vashti, were the perfect example. They had recently just started speaking after almost twenty years because Valerie married a black man, and the family was against it.

Valerie's parents, two siblings and their children had disowned them, but she stuck by her husband. And just as crazy people do, they thought when Vance was killed, Valerie would share her money with them.

*"Absolutely crazy,"* Veronica mumbled as she shook her head at the thought of her mother's kinfolk. *Had Mom listened to them and turned away from our dad, neither I, nor Vance, would be here.*

Veronica smiled and spoke aloud, "Thank God she had her own mind."

Unlike her maternal family members, she would close her mouth, keep her opinions to herself, and allow the Lord, Vance and Jasmine room to figure this thing out. And the one question she did ask—whether or not they had prayed about the move—was unavoidable. But still, who was she or anyone else, as a matter of fact, to go against anyone who said, "God gave them permission."

*Stranger things had happened, like Mary, a virgin, having a baby by the Holy Spirit when she was betrothed to Joseph.*

Veronica mumbled, "Now, if God could do that, who am I to say God wasn't in their plans. What right do I have to go against anything God was for." Veronica shook her head.

The thought of being cautioned all of her adult life about moving in with a guy was too deep to diminish or discard. Veronica surmised that she would just have to deal with how she felt with prayer. Her mom always said,

"Becoming a live-in with him will put too much stress on you to operate as a wife without having the benefits that come with the commitment."

*But then again, this is a new generation.*

Veronica began to compare her parents then, against her now. That generation figured if you bought the cow, then you had a right to its milk. And even if there were flaws in the beginning, with the help of the Lord, that would work out. This generation figures if you couldn't live together, how on earth would you be able to decide whether or not the person was a good fit for marriage.

It wasn't as if she and Kane hadn't discussed it before. Or debated both sides. They decided the caution against shacking was more about loving God enough to abstain from sex, especially when you had no safe-zone to run to. *Your own home.* Things did get heated when you date and one thing could lead to another. Quick. For them, sex was about the spiritual, even though, their generation made it about the natural. They both awaited the day they could sexually connect after marriage, but for now, they were happy to have their very own, safe-zone.

*Vance and Jasmine have to figure things out for themselves. Period.*

By the time her thought process of them ended, she'd finished all of her dusting and cleaning. Veronica scanned the room trying to locate her phone and spotted it on the table, right where she'd left it. Like normal, her mind was moving faster than her feet which caused her to stumble.

"Uggh. Thank you Jesus," she said, as she caught herself before falling.

Veronica picked up the phone, looked down at the time, and screamed, "Shoot!" It was six-thirty and she wanted to be in the office before seven-thirty. She quickly placed the phone back on the table and scurried to get in the shower.

*How in the world did I let time slip by me?*

She wouldn't be able to have her morning meditation time, not to mention her coffee. Frowning, Veronica raced to the bathroom, turned on the shower, dropped her robe, and quickly jumped in. She scrubbed her body good, rinsed off, and then carefully stepped out of the tub trying not to slip. Once both her feet were firmly and securely on the rug, she laughed and shook her head.

Clumsy should have been her middle name. And this morning she had no time to nurse a fall. Veronica carefully dried her body, slipped her feet in her slippers, and hurried to her bedroom.

The navy blue pantsuit and pink ruffled front blouse awaited her. *Lord, I need to hurry up and get to this job.*

Veronica dressed and then eyed herself in the mirror. *Professional and tasteful*, which was more than she could say about a lot of female realtors and contractors. Sometimes Veronica wondered if they had their day job confused with their night-time activities.

But she wasn't the dress police, and would never tell a grown woman how to dress. Although, the way she dressed and the manner in which she carried herself caused money to find her. So as long as she was on point, there was no need to downplay anyone else.

Veronica sat on her bed and slid her feet into the navy blue, red-bottomed, high-heeled pumps. She stood, looked at herself in the floor length mirror, and smiled. *Girl, you tight.*

"A glamour girl in a man's world, I am. I am." She picked up her navy leather Brahmin briefcase, stopped by the table to retrieve her phone, and headed for the front door. Veronica gave herself one last look-over in the foyer's mirror, nodded for self-approval, and went through her checklist..."Purse, keys, briefcase, Apple laptop, and lunch bag."

She pressed the four-digit alarm code, hit the AWAY button, and opened the door. As soon as she opened the door, her eyes immediately focused on the winter wreath she'd hung on Kane's door. "Beautiful, but I sure wish I was seeing his handsome face." She giggled and quickly closed her door. Sometimes, she felt she needed more than the thirty-seconds to exit the apartment before the alarm sounded. But today wasn't one of those days.

As she walked towards her car, her thoughts were on how much she really did miss Kane. Lately, she was also thinking of how much of a better choice he was for her than Rufus. Although it was hard not seeing him as such, she still couldn't complain. Her prayers were being answered. Business was booming, her coins were stacking, and she was working overtime trying to keep up with her assigned workload. *Praise God.*

Veronica loved her job, but with the new Stonewall area expanding, developers were using their company to build everything from houses to police stations. She was in demand, and to her surprise most of the developers requested her. *Another reason to praise God.*

Once she was in her car, she fumbled with the radio until she found XM64. She turned on the ignition and slowly backed out of the driveway. As the Williams Brothers sang, "Ooh wee, another blessing," she bobbed her head and sang along.

Once the song was over, she prayed aloud. "Lord, this is the day that You have made, I will rejoice and be glad in it. My soul shall make a boast unto You, oh Lord, keep me humble and make me glad. You are my hiding place and my heart's desire. Assign my angels over me, put them to work, but most of all cover me with Your blood. And thank you for another day, and another blessing, in Jesus' name. Amen."

# CHAPTER 3

J essica stood with her knee propped on her bedroom ottoman thinking about, Jasmine. Although, things still weren't back to normal, they were slowly getting back to pleasant. The day Jasmine told her and Jasper that she was leaving with Vance, Jasper blew a fuze. The dude could have had a heart attack or stroke as mad as he was. *But that still didn't stop me from giving him his issue.*

After a round or two, he finally came to himself, but it had left Jessica still buried in her thoughts and feeling broken. She always wondered how men could do things and then try to force everything back to normal, forgetting what they'd done. *You tried it Jasper, but not on my watch.* She wasn't God, but she surely wasn't going to allow him to be on a high horse, especially, when he, too, had fallen short of God's glory.

Jessica allowed her mind to drift back to that day and

their conversation. She would never have said some of the things she said to him in front of Jasmine. But as soon as their daughter exited the room, she let him have it in her mother-like fashion—until he saw the plank in his own eyes.

*"And you. I cannot believe you let our daughter walk out that door without saying anything. You—"*

*"You what, Jessica? Say it. You've been wanting to say what you've really felt for years, but you've been holding it back. Say what you really want to say."*

*"Don't push me, Jasper because we both know I can't stand a sanctimonious hypocrite. And she's right. See, all the times you were cheating on me and taking our children around those skanks affected them all in some sort of way."*

*"So we bringing that up now?"* Jasper screamed.

*"We sure are. The boys, were taught by me how to treat their wives, and whereas Jasmine should have been taught by you what to expect from a man, you were too busy showing her."*

*"I will not let you put this on me, Jessica!"* Jasper ranted.

*"You were big enough to smoke the pipe then, now stew in the residue of its smoke now. Your daughter does not want to jump and marry a man who may one day do what you did."*

*"Living together won't stop him."*

*"She's made her decision. Jasmine thinks this will allow her to see his true heart—before she jumps into a marriage. I'm not in agreement, but I will support my child."*

*"Even if she goes against what God said."*

*"The Bible says nothing about shacking but everything*

*about having self-control and refraining from passion or sexual immorality. So, what happened to you, Jasper? You failed and the same God you failed, gave you the same grace He's giving to your daughter."*

*"Really, Jessica."*

*"Really. You admitted to your lack of self-control. But Jasmine, she's committed to coming back home if living together becomes too much. Now, what more can you ask anyone for? I lived with you for two years before you got back in the bed with me. And the same God who sustained me—until you got your act together—can sustain our daughter."*

*"It's good to know that whenever I correct our children, I have to be given the list of my faults, Mrs. Good Mother."*

*"It's never been like that and you know it. Jasper, you have never looked at Jasmine or treated her like those boys, because to you she's the girl you never want a man to do like you did me. I get that. But you should have also remembered while you were in the streets that you reap what you sow. Now, is this your reaping season? Only God knows. But what I do know is you will not hold her to a standard that's hers alone."*

*"But Jessica, she's my only daughter. And I'm a man. I know how our body is made up. I know the things we think about, even when we don't want to think about it. I also know the power of temptation—whereas it concerns a man."*

*"But do you know the power of our God? She's my only daughter too, Jasper. I trust that even with our mistakes, we have raised her to never forget there is a God. Even when we do not trust God in ourselves, we must always trust the God we have put in our children. They won't always make the right*

decisions. *But they are protected by the same God. The One who told me if I was going to protect them, He'd move out of the way. But I told Him I'll move out of the way because my protection is not even a fraction of His. I'm out of the way of this, and so should you."*

*"I get it now, but you sure took some big jabs in order for me to get it. I don't like when you throw my past in my face."*

*"Well, my love, that's what happens when we do things outside of the will of God. They become like a bad tattoo we want to erase. You learn to live with your mess as a staple of why you'll never go that route again. You also remember that sometime, it's easy to get besides ourselves. We good for taking the plank off someone else's eyes, while living with blurred vision from our own planks. So every now and again, we need the friendly reminders then it becomes easier to help others remove their planks when ours are exposed and laying in front of us instead of on our eyes."*

*"You are such a wise woman and even though I want to throw a brick at you sometimes, I remember how wise you are and how much God has your back. I love you, Jessica, and thank you. Now, I need to go to my daughter and beg her pardon."*

*"Sounds like the Jasper Booth, Sr. I married thirty-some-thing-odd-years ago."*

*"You better believe I'm here, and I'm not going anywhere."*

Jessica rubbed her hand across her forehead and moved over towards her bed and sat on the corner. She loved the fact that no matter what time she'd called Jasmine at night, she was in her own room. It showed that they were trying to adhere to what they'd both been taught. *But will living saved prove harder than they thought?*

Both J.J. and Kane had been like Jasper, completely against the move. But after she had a long conversation with them, they decided to trust God in Jasmine. Jessica bowed her head. She'd been in her own head too long. It was now time to cast her cares on the Lord.

"Lord, I know we've done right by her and showed her your ways. Please don't allow the enemy to entice them with sex and don't let them make or not make the decision to marry because of what has happened in our past, in Jesus' name. Amen."

Jessica looked up at the sound of footsteps nearing her bedroom door. She focused on the door hoping it wasn't Jasper. Things were still a little awkward after their heated argument. They were back into their normal routine and had both apologized. Although he acted like the matter was behind them, she could still feel the strain from the situation.

She'd also apologized for making him feel as though she was still using his past against him. But that didn't erase the fact that he, like most men, never wanted to be confronted with what they wanted to vanish. But then again, had he never came for their child, she would have never said what she said.

Whether or not she was wrong, Jessica had still been praying daily for that answer. She never wanted to be right in her own eyes, but at the same time, causing her husband to feel less than a man. She also never wanted Jasper to ever feel like their children came before him.

She could still defend them, but not as if their dad was the enemy. And neither, by putting his position as the head of their household in jeopardy.

Because what would it profit her to belittle the man whom loved her enough to die for her. Or, even neglecting God's divine order for the family just to prove herself right. Neither would add any merits to her life and more than being right in an argument, she wanted to be right by God.

# CHAPTER 4

Rufus Burns sat at his desk, clasped his hands together, placed them behind his head, and leaned back in his chair. There were so many things running through his mind. The paper someone placed on the corner of his desk wasn't making matters any better. The headlines read…A Booth Wedding To Remember.

Rufus snatched up the "New Society Newspaper" and glared at the first photo he spotted. In a muzzled voice he read, "Jasper Booth Jr. and his new bride Jade Renee Booth." Squinting his nose as his left eyelid lifted in disgust, he folded the paper and hit the desk. His first mind was to toss it clean across the room, but curiosity overpowered him. He did as any curious person would do, Rufus opened the newspaper to Page 4 and began to read.

*Attorney Jasper Booth Jr. married the love of his life, Jade*

*Renee Bishop, now Booth. The ceremony which was held on Christmas Day became the most unforgettable event of the year.*

*The Booth family is not only a prominent Louisiana family but now one with Dade County connections.*

*Dade County's very own Valerie Kimbrel Booth, the late wife of Detective Vance Kimbrel Sr., is now married to the uncle of Jasper Booth J., Dr. James Booth. And looks like there are more fireworks between these two families to come. The next Kimbrel Booth wedding will feature Veronica Kimbrel. Our sources confirm that this wedding will be happening soon. New Society will be certain to get all the details of the upcoming nuptials and feature them right here.*

Rufus threw the newspaper in the trash beside his desk. *Dumb mother—*

Buzz, buzz.

His thought and profanity were interrupted by the buzzing of the phone. "What!" He answered still fuming from the article.

"What's wrong with you?" Selena asked.

"What, Selena? I'm at work. What have I told you about calling me in the middle of the day?"

"I was calling about the bank," she whined.

"We'll talk about that later. Bye." Rufus hung up in her ear without giving her time to say another word.

His mind went back to where he'd left off before Selena rudely invaded his thoughts. Veronica had another thing coming if she thought dissing him was going to be that easy. Sure, he'd done just what that Chief told him to do: he packed his bags and left Louisiana. Caddo was their turf, but Dade County was his.

He had a right to be pissed. Whatever happened on their turf should have stayed there, but his boss, Captain Lane, had questioned him about his trip. He even had the nerves to warn him if he did anything to meddle in Veronica's life, he would make his world a living hell. Rufus didn't take too kindly to threats, from anyone.

Valerie came to mind when he wondered who called. It really didn't make a difference. He was a grown man. No one in the department had even known he'd gone there, and all they had now was his word against theirs. But to him, it was a dead subject because his business had nothing to do with the department.

Rufus shook his head thinking about the confrontation with his boss. Most of the old heads loved the Kimbrel family and viewed Veronica and Vance as their very own children. They wanted for nothing after the death of their father. But there were also those who thought their father was the choice negro and got what he deserved.

But if they thought he was going to just die in the trenches—while she married another man—they all had another thing coming.

Especially, not after she'd made him get tied to her quack-job of a cousin, Selena. It was all Veronica's fault. Had she accepted his proposal, Selena would have always been just one of his thots. Her jealousy of Veronica made her quickly accept his marriage proposal. But turns out, he was the fool.

All she did was stay in his face complaining about anything she could find to complain about. If it wasn't about getting botox in her lips or a personal trainer for her butt, she was begging for him to cuddle. On top of her being an irritating headache, he was watching his seven-digit account magically disappear. *A loose broad, with a card.* But after today, she was in for a rude awakening.

Judging by the phone call, she'd already found out how much money was in her account. The account was all hers now because the joint-thing was over. Rufus snickered. "Now, she'll get a monthly allowance like a child, and if she goes through that money in a month, I'm putting her and her shoes on the street."

"What's so funny, Burns?" Sergeant Charleston asked Rufus as he walked by.

"Married life."

"Tell me about it. You should have left well enough alone."

"Nawl, I should have just taken what was mine." Rufus turned his attention back to his thoughts. *I've got to stop letting what's in my head, come out my mouth.*

He looked down at his buzzing phone again, but this time it was a text message.

*Boss, USCC playing Saturday in a championship game. Isn't Vance on that team? I do believe Veronica will be there. What about you? D2*

He didn't reply because he kept telling the dummies who worked for him that the first thing detectives did was pull phone records. He erased the message and leaned back in his chair. That nut might be on to something.

*But first I've got to deal with this trick and all her crap.*

Rufus thought about all the stuff that came with Selena. Hundreds of handbags and too many shoes and clothes to count. She'd nearly taken over his bedroom closet and now her stuff was all over his guest bedroom. He was disgusted this morning when he walked past the room, and Rufus did what any other man would, closed the door.

He had seemingly watched on the sidelines as his money and home were invaded by someone who didn't care one bit about his hard work. He put his life and his butt on the line to get the kind of money he had, and Rufus refused to allow her to wipe him out.

*This is about the dumbest move I could have ever made.*

She never cooked, cleaned, or did anything that would require breaking one of those expensive finger-nails. Nothing with Selena was done in moderation. She had her nails done more than he changed his mind.

*This is exactly why I wanted Veronica.*

She made her own coins, and hers were a mere frac-tion of what she made. He could have been the one buying Gucci leather loafers and four-hundred dollar Gucci belts. But nawl, now he had a fine babe with gold-digger tendencies. But the awakening was going to be

23

powerful enough to shake her until she recognized the power of Rufus.

He picked up his phone and the keys to his cruiser. It was time he paid a visit to D2. He'd come too far to let some uneducated, dope boy ruin his gig.

When he pulled up on the scene, the men scattered like a disturbed ant bed.

"D2 let me holler at you," Rufus lowered the passenger window and D2 stuck his head in the cruiser.

Wop! Wop! Wop! Rufus struck the young man three times quick with his club.

"I'm going to tell you for the last time. Don't ever leave me a text about anything. Do you understand?"

"Yes, boss," the young man said through tears, holding his head.

Rufus pulled off running over the young man's foot.

# CHAPTER 5

Jessica cleared her throat. "Lord, I've tried to be the best wife and parent that I can be."

She began to sob. Not because she felt like a failure. She just wished the Lord would have given detailed and line by line precepts on how to be both a wife and parents.

Jessica also wished the Lord would have given her direct instructions on how to navigate between the child and a parent. Especially in times like these. Now, she would just have to rely upon the Holy Spirit in hopes that He'd direct her and vindicate her at the same time.

*Lord, You never said what to do when the child became an adult and was old enough to make their own decisions.*

"Lord, You also never said that after we raised them, we had to stand on their necks making them do what's right. You said, 'Train up a child in the way he shall go and when he is old, it will not depart from him.'"

For Jessica, that meant that eventually they will come back to what they know is right and biblically sound to do. At least, that is what she hoped.

Her thoughts were again interrupted but this time by three knocks on the door and then she heard Valerie's voice, "Sis, are you in there?"

"Come in, Valerie."

"How are you holding up?"

"Girl, things are better, but my mind is still stuck on our two crazy children."

"I've done my best to train Vance in the ways of the Lord, and I told the Lord years ago, if I gave him to You like I said I did, please help me not to worry.'"

"You have a valid point."

"I know I do. I promise you, I sleep at night. James tried to start up about the situation."

"That's Jasper's brother so I can only imagine how he felt."

"Well, no need. I told him, 'cast his cares on the Lord, not me.' Sis, I've learned many are dead because they tried to handle things and people that belonged to God. I refuse to lose a minute of sleep or not even one of these gray hairs on my head worrying about either of my children, or now, my husband. I promise our God is big enough."

"You're right, He is. I don't know what's gotten into me. Jasper had me all in knots."

"Men will do that, but you have to know what you know and stand on it."

"I know we raise these children, and that doesn't mean they will always do as they were taught. But one thing is for sure, the same God who protected us will do the same for them."

"Amen. Now you're talking like my sister."

"This stuff has a way of choking you out and then make you second guess everything you know is right. I was just telling God that I wish He would have given me line by line directions."

"And we still wouldn't have followed them. The enemy is cunning and he'll nag us to think it's all about us. Or either how people will look at us. In reality, it's not about us at all. It's all about God. And if this is His route, and if He would allow this, who are we to go against the lesson they will learn."

"Cause there will be a lesson, won't there?"

"As sure as my name is Valerie Booth, and I'm standing here talking to Jessica Booth," Valerie rolled her eyes. "God is up to something in their lives. And I'm just going to stand right here on the sidelines and keep praying that their faith fails not. And also that the Lord doesn't take His hands of protection from over them."

"You've said a mouthful right there, honey. I am so glad you are in my life and that we have one another."

"Jessica, me too. Although, I questioned if James and I were moving too fast."

"You did?"

"Yes, but

I found peace with the fact that we'd be sisters even if he and I didn't work."

"Wow, that's special, Valerie, but you guys will work."

"Vashti and I wasted so much time fighting opinions until we lost what sisterhood was about. Now, God has given me you, and also put her back in my life. I'm feeling like the most blessed woman in Louisiana."

"You are surely blessed, but the most, I'd have to take that to a judge, honey. And all because if I look back over all He's brought me through, my soul would argue you down that you and no one else could out do me as Mrs. Blessed."

"One thing I know, He's been faithful and the same thing He's done for others, He's done for us."

"Amen. Now let's go find us something to chew on. You know when you come back to life, the first thing you want is food."

"I'm right behind you sister. And hey, don't let nothing bring you to the point of emotional death again. God has you and all the issues you'll ever come against." Valerie hugged Jessica.

"You've said a mouthful sis," and they headed towards the kitchen.

# CHAPTER 6

K ane unbuttoned his four-button suit jacket, pulled it off, and hung it on the coat hanger next to the bookshelf. Stretching his body, he twisted side to side, lowered his arms and slowly walked back towards his desk. Although his mind was excited about what the new day would bring, his body wanted nothing more than a few hours of sleep.

He yawned, sat in his chair, and opened his top desk drawer to retrieve some files.

"Shoot!" he said as a stack of pictures toppled on the floor. Kane pushed back from his desk and bent over to retrieve the photographs. Placing them on top of his desk, he scooted himself back to the perfect position. He needed to get back to work and find what he went in the drawer for in the first place, but something beckoned him to go through the pictures—one by one.

Kane smiled.

The wonderful wedding photos of his brother J.J. to his first and only love Jade made him feel overjoyed. It was a Christmas wedding to remember, captured by almost every society newspaper. He looked at each photo but when he got to one, his heart melted. It was his future bride Veronica with her head laying on his shoulder.

"My Veronica," he whispered. Her hair, smile, attentiveness, and even her voice made him happy to be her man. The one God created just for her.

*Absolutely magical. The entire wedding.*

But for Kane, the real magic happened the day after the Christmas wedding…his birthday. He just knew J.J. and Jade would leave right after the wedding. But to his surprise, they chose to celebrate his birthday before leaving. If Kane never knew how J.J. felt about him as a big brother, that was the *'tell-all'* and testament of his love.

Kane swiped a tear with one finger and nodded.

Now, all he had to do was hold the fort down—in their office—until J. J. came back. And with the help of his mother, make sure that Veronica's wedding day was just as special.

He'd never top J.J.'s surprise wedding to Jade. Only an over-the-top romantic could make a woman so tearful, she nearly froze at the top of the aisles. But, after seeing how special the Booth clan does things, Veronica agreed to let him be the mastermind of their wedding.

Kane wasn't like J.J. when it came to romance, so he did what any smart guy would do, he employed J.J. and his mother Jessica to do all the planning. All he wanted to do was sign the checks. And with Valentine's on the horizon, they all figured it would be the perfect occasion to shock Veronica. What was even better, Valentine's Day fell on a Friday.

A Friday night wedding for a woman who had already picked her wedding dress. But little did she know, they would only use that dress for the sake of staged photos. Mrs. Jamecia, the owner of Jourdain's Boutique, was creating the perfect red gown for the woman of his dreams.

And if it fits anything like Jade's dress, he would have to definitely keep himself and all his members under the rule of self-preservation through self-control.

*"Okay, Jackson-Booth, put the photos down and get the wedding stuff off your mind."*

He moved some files, folders, and envelopes around in his bottom drawer until he found an unused golden envelope. Kane inserted all the pictures inside and wrote on the front in large letters—J.J. & Jade's Wedding.

He shoved the pictures back in his top desk drawer. Kane made a note on a yellow sticky notepad to have his assistant buy a photo album so the pictures could be displayed in the lobby. Jessica had prints made to give clients who didn't make the guest list. She also wanted a book made to give them an opportunity to see the wedding. And if Jessica Booth came to their office and didn't see those pictures in the lobby, Kane already knew what kind of fit she'd have.

Kane pushed the button on the Intercom.

"Hope, would you please come to my office for a moment?"

"Yes, Sir. I'll be there shortly."

Hope Gatlin had become an invaluable help to their law office. Kane could never imagine why someone hadn't already hired her because not only was she brilliant, she was kind and resourceful.

"How can I help you, Mr. Jackson-Booth?"

"How many times do I have to tell you to call me Kane? I'm Kane in the office and Jackson-Booth or Jackson or Booth whenever we are before clients, only."

"I know, I'm just trying to get used to things."

"You are doing an excellent job, Hope, and I'm for one glad you were exactly where God needed you to be when we found you. Now, I'm trying to find the Kimbrel files. Have you seen them?"

"Yes, Mrs. Harris pulled them from your office on Monday. Let me see if she's finished with them."

"No, that's okay. I'll call her in a few. Thanks, again, and keep up the good work."

"Yes, Sir." Hope turned to leave and then thought of something else. "Ms. Kimbrel called and she said that she won't be able to make lunch, but dinner is on her tonight."

"Thank you," Kane said with a grimace, "And Hope..."

"Yes." She turned back to face him.

"Would you or Mrs. Harris please go out and get a

photo album so you can place the wedding photos out in the lobby?"

"No problem. Where are the photos?"

"They will be in this envelope in my top drawer. I don't want to release them until you all have something for certain to put them in. If my hunch is correct, Jessica Booth will be walking in this office soon and if she doesn't see those pictures in the lobby..."

"You are going to get the issue," Hope finished with what he considered slang for a good lashing.

"Exactly. You've only been here for a couple of weeks and you already know our mother. When she wants something done, everyone in the vicinity of her eyes gets busy. She has an authority that I've never seen on anyone except her."

"Yes, Sir. She doesn't play any games. And you're right, when she comes in here and starts talking, I forget who my real bosses are. Jessica Booth becomes my head boss." Hope laughed. "I'm on it right now, boss." She made air quotes as she spoke and then turned to leave, pulling the door closed behind her.

Kane laughed.

HOPE HAD ONLY BEEN THERE a little while, and she already knew his mom. Jessica was a force all by herself. Sort of just like the woman he found. His mind drifted back to Veronica, the love of his life. He made a mental note to go by the beauty supply to buy some foot scrub so he could soak her feet.

These days, Dwight Esplanade's Construction was just as busy as the Law Offices of Jackson & Booth. Thanks to new developers and people selling, Veronica had been busy since January.

Kane wasn't at all surprised by her not being able to make their lunch date. As a matter of fact, he was not sure if he'd make it either. Things were picking up in their office and now they had a client who was not only family—his aunt by marriage—but soon to be his mother-in-love.

Their firm had taken on Veronica's mother as a client and trying to sort through some details from her father's estate that had seemingly gone undone. But one thing was for sure, with Jackson and Booth on the case, they were going to find out all the information, that needed to be discovered.

# CHAPTER 7

Veronica had such a huge pile of stuff awaiting her, until she almost wanted to turn around and go back home. Plans, plans, plans. And no one else in the office wanted to approve or revamp them. She'd gotten used to doing all the things the men hated doing, but her mind was made up this year to use a word she rarely used: N-O.

It had nearly shocked one of her coworkers still—when he asked her to make the coffee—and she told him, "No."

She was just as much an engineer as he was and he'd left his wife at home, and it was high time he learned that. The only time she would make the coffee is if she wanted some and none was in the coffee pot already. From now on, she was only accountable to herself, her boss, and job.

She wasn't going to neglect her obligations because

how would she ever get her own if she didn't prove faithful with the business of her boss? Her daddy taught her that. He would always say, "When you have proven yourself faithful over another man's stuff, that's when God will bless you with your own."

But *good steward* didn't mean being stupid.

Nor did it mean doing things you had the right to say, "No," to. Like making coffee and going to get wives gifts' and flowers because their husband thought his coworker picked better gifts than him. She never wanted her future husband to have someone else buying her gifts. Especially his female co-workers. Doing unto others, what she didn't want done to her, was over.

Veronica sorted through the plans on her desk putting the ones she would tackle on the right and those she would hand back to the engineer—who *should* be looking over them—to the left. After she'd got her stack down to five plans, she got up from her desk and went straight to Dwight's office.

Veronica knocked on his door and only entered when she heard him say, "Come in."

"Hey, Esplanade. These are the plans of some of your lazy employees, and I believe it would be beneficial for you to give them back to them, instead of me."

"It's about time you wised up. I've been watching you run around here like Girl Friday and I prayed that one day you'd figure out that they were skating whilst you were rock climbing."

"Why do men do that?"

"Because you are a woman who has it going on around here. You can do your load and theirs, and you never complain. They don't mind you making more money than them as long as you're doing something for them."

"The devil is a liar."

"That he is. But you empower him when you allow slick people to think they got you just where they want you. Now, my good mind says to let you put this right back on their desk, but my wise mind says it's time for me to step in. So, with that said, meet me in the board room in twenty minutes."

"I'll be there."

"Okay, but you do know when I put something on your desk, it's another story."

"Yeah, yeah, yeah." She laughed. "You are the best boss, and I know you'll never put something on my desk that you can do yourself. You only mess with me when you get stuck and need an extra set of eyes, and I appreciate you for that. That's why I do everything I do for Dwight Esplanade's Constructions as unto the Lord. I know God will bless me, like He blessed me with this job and like He's blessed me with the best boss in you."

"Girl, get out of here before you make me shout. I've been asking God to make me a good boss and set a guard over my lips because wifey says, "Dwight you just say anything."

"She's right, but I've noticed you're getting better. You

aren't walking around here cussing those dudes out as much as you used to."

"Yeah, I've been threatening to fire two of them for years, and I can't keep using my mouth for empty threats. I think the frustration of trying to help them stay employed makes me cuss. But Jayla keeps telling me that blessings and cussing don't come out of the same mouth."

"The Bible says, 'cursing,' but the foul language is just as bad as cursing someone to what you've called them. I promise I have to pray for my mouth because being here every day and listening to you all, can taint a lady. I keep praying for the Lord to set a guard over these lips."

"I feel you, Kimbrel."

"Well, I'll see you in fifteen now."

"Perfect."

Veronica walked out of Dwight's office feeling empowered. She was getting her life back and on track. She refused to bring old hiccups and baggage into a marriage with Kane. He deserved a woman who was able to leave not just some of her past, but all of things behind her including the isms and mess that stunts growth. And today was a huge step towards obeying her own man.

Veronica stepped into her office and stood still for a moment.

*Kane told me someone else sees what's been happening and I had no idea Dwight's been watching all along.*

It wasn't long before she, nine other engineers and Dwight's secretary, Felecia Smith, were flocked around the huge cherry wood conference table. Right after

opening prayer, Dwight lit into the men so fierce
Veronica felt bad for them.

"All these plans are plans you lazy bums dropped on
Kimbrel's desk as if she's your personal secretary or
maid. From this day forward, you need my permission to
take anything to her or even across the threshold of her
office door. Am I understood?

"And, Veronica Kimbrel, you better not take another
plan that doesn't belong to you, unless I bring it to you.
For months, these good gentlemen have used you and
felt justified because next to me, your money is the
second highest. And that's from hard work...not because
you are a woman and I decided to give you more than
them. Kimbrel works her butt off and instead of you
guys appreciating the business that she brings to this
company, and praising her for it, you hate. The spirits of
envy and jealousy are too strong to stay hidden, and if
you can't deal with the way things are, by all means,
there's the door."

Jason Hayes clapped his hands.

"Jason, since you are the only one who appreciates
what I'm saying, I'm giving you a five-thousand dollar
bonus today. Mrs. Smith," Dwight called to his secretary
who was taking notes of the meeting.

"Yes, sir," she answered.

"Write Hayes a check for five-thousand dollars. God
told me to sow into someone's life and Hayes when you
clapped your hands as the others frowned, the Lord said
the blessing needed to fall on you."

39

You could tell by the look of strain on a couple of the men's faces, they hated they didn't join in with Hayes.

Hayes was praising the Lord as if he was in church. He was praising so hard until Veronica said, "Wow." She and Ms. Smith began to cry.

"I feel you, brother. Because God will bless you in the most unusual places, at the most unusual times. He will use a moment of reprimand to show your humility and bless you in the midst of those too hard-hearted to obey or either embrace what it said."

"You just don't know," Jason said.

"Yes, I do. Things have not always been like this for me, but one thing I know, if you do right by others, God will do right towards you. Now, let's move on. Is there anyone in here who needs a letter of recommendation for another company?"

Mitchell Andries stood.

# CHAPTER 8

**J**anuary 24, Los Angeles. Vance pulled off his practice uniform and headed for the showers. Once the water temperature was good, he turned on his waterproof radio and jumped in. He figured, by the time the reporter talked to the other two seniors, he'd be done and ready for his interview.

"Kimbrel, she's waiting on you," one of his teammates called out to him.

"On the way," he responded.

He never liked talking about the upcoming games because only the Lord knew who would win. He had one obligation…to protect the quarterback. Seemingly, since he'd done so well at that, he was sure to be a first or second round draft pick.

"There you are, Mr. Kimbrel," Elaina Mitchell smiled.

Vance gave her a dry-like smile because she knew as well as he did they weren't friends. She just happened to be his first college girlfriend who'd slept with his team-mate and was now doing everything in her power to win him back.

It was over.

"Okay, let's get this done."

"What's the hurry? She waiting for you to call her or something?"

"She's none of your business, and if you don't do whatever it is you waited on me to do, then you'll be standing here looking crazy."

"Vance Kimbrel, what are your plans for the championship game tomorrow?"

"Many are the plans of man, but it is the Lord's plans that prevails. If the Lord is willing, we will be empowered to come against such a wonderful team, but also come away with a 'W.'"

"We understand that scouts from all over will be checking you out tomorrow. Will that affect your game?"

"Of course not. I have a team to support and it's never about me. Again, my future has already been set in stone by the Almighty. If He opens doors for me, I'll walk in. So why should I be afraid if God is for me? He's more than the world against me."

"There's a lot riding on this championship game for your teammates who are seniors, and also, yourself. We are rooting for you to do your very best."

"That's all we can give...our best," Vance smiled and turned to leave.

"Not so fast, Mister. And what about me? Are you going to hold what I did against me forever?"

"Elaina, we are done. You already know this, and there's nothing more to talk about. I'm engaged to be married and you do know that as well, too."

"Whatever. Like I said, will you hold what I did against me forever?"

"Actually, I forgave you a long time ago. Just not enough to deal with you again. We good though."

"Vance, if we were good you'd have your lips planted on mine right now." She grabbed the towel around his neck and pulled him so quickly into a kiss that he nearly lost his balance.

"Really, Elaina? He knew not to put his hands on her because he'd probably be framed for assaulting her. He stepped back, glared at her, threw the towel on the ground, and turned to walk away.

"Vance, Vance. Don't walk away from me."

"I did before and I'm doing it right now." He kept walking until he was back in the locker room with his team.

❧

ONE MIND TOLD him to ask his coach if he could call Jasmine so he could tell her what just happened. He never wanted any secrets between them and these days, people were a bit more snakier than usual.

Social media gave them even more grounds to be

wicked, and he didn't need Elaina or her goons doing anything to hurt Jasmine.

Things were moving so fast in the locker room until after his name had been called a couple of times, he'd forgotten about the entire situation. Tomorrow would be the turning point of his life. If they won the National Championship, he was a sure upper round draft pick. If not...he'd go, but not with the proof position five to six digits he wanted to make.

Vance made his way to the eating room and sat down by his teammate Austin.

"Man, you look mad as crap."

"You'll never guess what Elaina did."

Austin turned his head and puckered his lips, "Yes, I would, but for the record, did you hit her?"

"Man, you know I'd never hit a chick. I wanted to slap her, but I just pushed myself back. She grabbed me by my towel and pulled me down into a kiss, which shocked me. These females are so aggressive and then will be the first to say you assaulted them."

"I know, right. But as Moms told me, the best method to stop abuse is getting in your car and leave."

"I just threw the towel on the ground and did just that. She better be glad I ain't like these other dudes who would hit that and still marry someone else. I thank God for self-control and consideration."

"Yeah, you aren't like some of us because believe me, I'd hit that thang and kick her out my house the next day in her underwear."

"See, that's why I pray for you, dude."

"Quit doing that, man, until I'm ready to change."

"Nawl, I can't. I love you like a brother, so I can't stop praying for you."

"I guess thanks is in order."

"It is. Now come on let's get in this line before all the food is gone."

"Right behind you, Vance."

ELAINA WALKED to her car smiling. *He thinks he's done something, but when I finish with him, he's going to wish he never met me.*

"What do I need to do?" The cameraman who was walking a couple of steps behind Elaina asked.

"Send me the footage and make a separate clip of the kiss."

"Got it."

"And make sure I have it within the next hour."

"Okay, Elaina."

She got in her car, backed out of the parking space, and headed in the direction of her apartment. Vance Kimbrel was going to pay for treating her like she was nothing. Right when he getting ready to receive his reward, she was going to show the world his real reward. A kiss from her.

She and the camera staff had put together a slideshow to run at the end of the game if USCC won and it would be the perfect time to put him on his knees.

*He thinks he loves the Lord and to pray. He's going to have to use every prayer in him to keep his little Ms. Perfect Jasmine. She's going to hate the day she came on my turf acting as if she was entitled to Vance. He belongs to me.*

Elaina made it home and picked out the best outfit in her closet. She needed to be dressed to the nines so when her video showed, they'd be looking at the queen herself. Nothing shabby. And definitely nothing short of perfection.

"This will be a night that no one will forget and I am going to be the star of the show."

# CHAPTER 9

"Mitchell, I was praying that you were man enough to stand. You'll have your letter within the next ten minutes and that should be all the time you'll need to clean your desk out and vacate these premises.

"Mrs. Smith, make that happen please."

Dwight looked from engineer to engineer before he spoke.

"If anyone of you doesn't like how I run my company, now is the time for you to leave as well. I have given my all to make this a premier construction company. We have some of the best engineers in the state of Louisiana, and also some of the best construction labor teams on earth. But if the head is broken, then you cannot expect the tail to be right.

"Do you all understand?"

"Yes, boss," the engineers answered.

"I will not ask either of you to give what I will not give. Neither will I ask you to do what I won't do. I am asking you to remember that in everything we do, we must do it as the Lord is the one who is inspecting us. Not man, but God. Do any of you have any questions?"

No one said anything.

"Okay, so since none of you said or asked anything, I don't want to hear about this meeting in being in gossip sessions. Of course, you can talk to your family. But after today, it's done. It's time to move forward. We wish Mitchell the best and after today, he is none of our business. Amen."

"Amen," the staff answered.

"Let's pray. Father, we thank you for blessing this business, this team, and all of our crews. We know that all things work together for our good, so we thank you for all things, both the good and the bad. Continue to bless the works of our hands, and we will continue to bless You, in Jesus' name. Meeting adjourned."

❦

AFTER THE MEETING ADJOURNED, Veronica could not wait to get back to her desk so she could call Kane. She had to tell him about the unexpected office meeting.

Sure, she knew Dwight appreciated her, but never in a million years did she think it was enough to defend her as he did.

The room was full of swarming men when Dwight

was giving Andries his walking speech. Mitchell was a good engineer but his level of pride far out-weighed his abilities to produce architecture. So many clients complained about his lack of listening and, to be honest, most of the team wanted him gone.

Not Veronica.

She knew how hard it was to be a family without a working father. Losing his job was the last thing she would have suggested. But in all reality, he'd messed his own self up. The same pride that caused him to stand up in that meeting, was the same pride that now had him searching for a job.

He and Rufus Burns were one and the same.

Seemingly cut from the same cloth.

Two men, who had great potential, but were too caught up in their abilities and themselves. Both too blind to realize that everything they had came from the One above. And both suffocating their potential in a pool of pride.

Veronica put her tablet on the desk, sat in her seat, and immediately picked up the phone to dial the law office.

"Law offices of Jackson and Booth. How may we assist you?"

"Hello, Hope. How are you?

"Hello Veronica, I'm good and you?"

"All is well, may I please speak with Kane?"

"Just a second and I will put you through," Hope hit

the buzzer on the phone and made the announcement, "Kane, it's Veronica."

"Put her through, please."

"You got it."

After the phone rang once, Veronica smiled as she listened to Kane's singing.

"Hello, hello, beautiful girl?"

"Kane, you always make me blush, but listen, stop singing. You will never believe what just happened."

He could hear the excitement in her voice that made him put all jokes aside. "What's up, Babe?"

"When I arrived this morning, the guys had so many files on my desk until it made me angry. Well, I marched those files right to Dwight and put them on his desk. Come to find out, he was just waiting for me to get enough. He called a meeting."

"Are you serious?"

"Dude, as a heart attack. I had no idea what the meeting would be about, other than, he needed them to stop giving me their work."

"Okay, did he handle that?"

"Did he? That dude told them why I made more money and that from this day forward they were to put nothing on my desk unless they brought it to him. Then, he would give it to me and not them. He chewed them out, Babe. I felt sorry for them, but happy at the same time."

"Girl, you better put that feeling sorry stuff in a can. Use it only when someone is in need of real compassion.

I told you men will use you up if you let them. This
doesn't just apply to the bed but all across the line."

"I always just thought they valued my opinion. Come
to find out, they were using me. I almost wanted to quit."

"For what? You're good at what you do, Veronica, and
there's no need in giving any place to the devil. Keep
doing what you do, and always do it to the glory of God.
He will continue to bless you and keep you on the top."

"But, Kane, you do know I do all and everything as
unto the Lord. And, I want to be able to help my co-
workers, but I don't want to be played."

"No one does. Love, it's easier for some people to feel
better about themselves when they are hurting others. Is
it God's way? Of course not, but His way seems to get
lost behind opinions, revenge, envy, jealousy, and pride."

"It surely does, doesn't it?"

"Yes. So, we must remember to always 'do unto others
as we would have them do unto us,' and listen to the Holy
Spirit. Don't just help because you feel like that will make
you look good. Help because you know you are God's
hands on the earth."

"Amen. Well, I need to get some things done before
we fly out tomorrow. I love you, Kane."

"I love you, Vee. And, Babe, make sure you don't
blame yourself for anything that happened today. You
did what any employee should have done and I'm proud
of you."

"You know they say, 'snitches get stitches,' but I'm not
definitely not taking any stitches."

"Okay, my little snitch. Talk to you later."

"Whatever." She hung up thinking at least she had a trip and a long weekend.

Away from the office.

Away from what happened.

A moment of escape filled with football and fun.

CHAPTER 10

**J**anuary 25th. J.J. and Jade flew in and the entire Booth family boarded the private airplane of Dr. Reginald Strong, at the Shreveport Downtown Airport. Reginald was the brother-in-love of First Lady Destiny, who was good friends and business partners with Kane. He cheerfully gave of his airplane to be used anytime Kane or his family needed it.

Kane could tell by the look in Veronica's eyes that she was impressed. The interior of the aircraft was nothing less than extravagant. There were white leather seats with the letter S inscribed on each. The white leather sofa on the right side of the plane extended from the front to the middle of the plane. And inscribed on the back of the sofa was the name Strong.

A dark cherry wood table separated the main sofa from five recliners. There was two other sections of seats in clusters of fours that had their very own individual tables, a small screen television with gaming devices, dvds, and headphones. There was a two-seat section in the back that was designed for the owner and his wife and gave them complete privacy from anyone else on board. Big screen televisions hung in the front and rear of the plane, but each seat was designed with its very own miniature screen and laptop.

As with everything else she'd designed, Destiny Strong had pulled no stops with the decorations in the plane. And if you knew her work, the entire plane screamed, Dobrielle's.

"Veronica, would you like to follow me to the back?"

"Baby, I'm sitting wherever you lead me."

"And, family, please sit where you'd like."

"You don't have to tell us, and we weren't waiting on you to approve either," Jessica Booth told her oldest son.

"I know, Mom. Have it your way."

"Indeed. Now, Kane, how long is this flight going to be?"

"About a five-hour flight, baby." Jasper Sr. answered, interrupting his son's response. Then patted his wife on the knee. "It's going to be over before you know it, and I've made sure you'll be fully entertained."

"And just what did you do, Jasper?"

"I made sure Kane brought that new movie by Jennifer Lopez and that *Girl's Trip* movie you like so much."

"You're alright with me, husband."

"I know what my wifey likes."

"Would you two can all the mushy talk already?" J.J. said frowning at his parents who were seated across the table from him and his new bride, Jade.

"You just wait until y'all been married as long as we have," Jessica shook her finger at J.J. "You'll use every opportunity to flirt with her, I promise."

"Yeah, son, sometimes it's best. When you get our age, all you can do is flirt."

"Speak for yourself, Jasper. I'm still holding my husband down in every way."

"You sure are, baby, and I love you for all that you do."

"Please, J.J., you know that these two can get started," Kane yelled from the back.

"Aw, you just sit back there and be quiet, Kane."

"J.J, you're just mad Vee and I beat you to these private quarters back here."

"Exactly." Everyone started laughing at J.J's eager confession. "And I call dibs on the way back."

"Dude, what are we? Ten again?" Kane countered.

"Nawl, just plain ole brothers."

"You're right about that, J.J." Jessica added, before looking around to face Valerie. "Have you heard from Vance, Sis?"

"He called yesterday before practice but said he had to turn in his phone and wouldn't be able to call me. I think Coach is really strict about them talking before their games."

"Most coaches are," James interrupted.

"I can definitely understand why." Jessica shook her head. "Prayerfully, they'll get the win."

"That's my prayer too, Jessica," Valerie agreed.

"So ladies, can we watch the movie now? By the time it finishes, we should be close if not already at the airport."

"Yes, Jasper," Jessica answered, patting her husband on the leg. If it were just the two of them, she wouldn't have been so polite since he was trying to shut her up. But today, he had a pass.

❧

JUST AS JASPER SAID, as soon as the movie went off, the pilot came over the speaker telling them to put on their seat belts. Each of them, even those who had nodded for a nap, awakened and obeyed.

Jessica looked around the airplane at her family.

"What?" Jasper Sr. asked his wife, knowing well the look on her face.

"I just got a revelation, Jasper."

"I felt that. I knew something had happened. I could see the look in your eyes. What did God show you?"

"He said, 'There will come a time when His children must wake up and obey.'"

"My God," Valerie cried out. "Lord, help me to wake up from anything I've been slumbering through and obey You. I just want to do Your will, Lord."

And just like that, the entire family broke out in praise.

Valerie began to pray. "Father, we call You, Abba. We cry out to You now. You are and am at the same time, the same God. We honor You. Lord, we don't want to sleep on You. When You move, God, we want to move. We want to be so sensitive to Your move, and so obedient to Your voice. Whatever You command, we will obey. Overtake us with Your spirit of obedience. For we know Your voice and we follow only You and You alone, in Jesus' name. Amen."

By the time the plane landed, they were still thanking and praising God.

Jade noticed J.J. crying as she'd never witnessed him cry, and as she wiped his eyes she began to sing. "We feel You moving, we feel You moving in this place. We feel You moving, We feel You moving in this space. And we welcome You."

J.J. fell to his knees as others were already kneeling.

Veronica began to back up Jade and she started singing, "Move Lord, move Lord. Move Lord, move Lord. In my mind move, in my heart move, in my will move, and in my worship move."

Jasper Sr. rose to his feet. "Father, I lift up my family before You, dear Master. In this unusual space, You have showered us with Your presence, You have moved. Father, I know without a doubt, there's a victory in Your presence. Move over circumstances and situations. Move Lord.

Because when You move, things change. Demons disappear. Fear vanishes. And, Your Word is made alive. It shall not return unto You void, and it will accomplish in the thing in which You have sent it. Let Your Word move on us, over us, through us, and for us, in Jesus' name we pray. Amen."

"I don't know what we are about to face, but one thing I know, the Lord has given us everything we needed through the glory He has placed in us in this space." Uncle James said as he held up holy hands.

"Hallelujah. Glory to God," Kane praised.

After the Spirit lifted, the family was back to laughing and joking. By the time the limo driver made it to the hangar, they were all refreshened and excited about the game. They had felt a move of God that brought restoration and replenishment.

# CHAPTER 11

*anuary 25th, Inglewood, California.* Jasmine stood
patiently at the ticket gate waiting for her family.
She was excited that all of them, including her dad,
decided to attend Vance's championship game.

The atmosphere was charged. People were chanting
and laughing as so many adorned the colors of cardinal
and gold. She'd seen how electric a college campus could
be, but to her, none ever compared to her alma mater's
Death Valley. But today the Trojins were definitely
ignited and coming in close throwing those two fingers
in the air for victory.

Just as she spotted her family, she also spotted the
female who had the potential to be the most problematic
for her. Elaina Mitchell. Her smile faded and was
replaced by Jasmine's *I wish you would* face. As usual, the
girl cringed her nose and walked right past her, but this

time, she wore a superficial grin that made Jasmine instantly mad.

"What's with the look? I thought you'd be happy to see us," Jasper Sr. said as he approached his daughter.

"Dad, I am. Hey y'all. I'm so happy to see you." Jasmine raced from person to person with a huge hug and kiss.

"Hello, my sweet darling daughter, Jasmine." Jessica greeted her baby. "I've missed you so much."

"And so have we," Jade retorted.

Jasmine gave Jade the side-eye, grinned, and then asked, "How was your honeymoon, chick?"

"Later conversation for a later date." Jade rolled her neck and wiggled her finger.

"You know I've missed you guys so much. Now let's go in here so you can get your tickets." Jasmine moved to the side to allow first her parents and then her aunt and uncle to pass. When everyone was in the line, both Veronica and Jade cornered her.

"What was that look about, Missy?" Jade put her hands on her hip.

"So, Elaina."

"Elaina Mitchell, Vance's ex-girlfriend," Veronica finished.

"Yes, her. She just passed by me with this sneaky vindictive grin on her face. I haven't been here a good full month, and this girl has made me want to strangle her."

"Well, one thing I know about my brother he's faithful, and she was anything but. So, you don't even have her to worry about." Veronica rubbed Jasmine on the shoulder.

"I know but you know how you feel something about someone and the feeling just—"

"Feel like a snake is near?" Veronica interjected.

"Yeah. That. She makes my skin crawl and although I know Vance has been home with me whenever he's not on lockdown, I just smell a rat."

"Okay, Kane," Veronica yelled out as Kane and J.J. beckoned she and Jade to come to get in line.

As they walked away, Valerie grabbed Jasmine's hand. "How is my future daughter-in-love?"

"Awe, Auntie, I'm doing well. I'm happy to see you all because I really do miss you guys." Jasmine had decided to continue calling Valerie auntie until she and Vance were officially married.

"We miss you all too. At least this is his last college game, and you'll be able to move closer to home as he trains."

"Yeah, I'm looking forward to that."

"I am too," Jessica said, coming up behind them. "Girl, I didn't realize how many times we did lunch together until you were gone. I miss it."

"Me, too, Mom. But you do know as soon as I get back, it's on once again."

"I can't wait, and this time we're dragging Valerie along."

"Jessica, you must not see these hips. Latino women

are just like black women, and too much food goes straight to this here." Valerie pointed at her butt.

"That surely won't disappoint me at all," James said, coming up behind Valerie and wrapping his arms around his wife.

"Really, Uncle James? Go over there with Dad and the guys and behave."

"Yes, ma'am, niece. But I'm just telling the truth."

"That's what I'm afraid of," Valerie responded.

"Veronica just tried to tell me a little about Elaina. What has she done?"

"Auntie, she hasn't had the opportunity to do anything because my bodyguard Vance is treating me like a celebrity. She just gives these *Girl, I hate you* looks."

"Well, she made her own bed, and now she's feeling some sort of way. That's a crazy woman for you," Valerie said.

"I'm just so grateful that Vance is so attentive to me, and he has made sure that I'm respected. I couldn't ask for anything more." Jasmine smiled and grabbed her daddy's stretched out hand.

"Baby girl, I'm so sorry I allowed you to think that I'm disappointed in you. You have, your entire life, made me so proud to call you daughter. Now, I didn't like this decision, still don't, but I love you. And, seeing you smile like you are smiling right now, makes me believe that Vance is the right choice for you."

"Thank you, Daddy."

As they made their way through the crowds at SoWi

Stadium, Jasmine beamed with excitement. She had her family, her man, and she was convinced that today, USCC would have the win. Life was exciting and nothing short of what she hoped it would be.

For now, she was pushing all the negativity behind her. She was getting ready to cheer her man into a victory from the fifty yard line, third row seats they had.

◈

WHEN THE TEAM ran from the tunnel and to the sidelines, Vance had his mind on nothing but the "W." He had a job to do, and he needed to get it done. Most of the team was hyped off the rapper Eminem's, "Til I Collapse," but before every game, Vance only listened to Tina Turner's "The Best." His mind was wired a whole entirely different way than most of his teammates. And that song used the perfect words to describe who he was on the field...the best.

As the team all came to the sidelines for the singing of the National Anthem, Vance looked into the stands and stole a peak of Jasmine and their family. They were all here, including her father, to support him and he couldn't be more happier.

*Get your head in the game V. Go out here and protect your quarterback.*

Vance closed his eyes and thanked the Lord for the opportunity to be playing in a championship game. Then he thanked the Lord for his family and friends.

"Lord, let Your will be done," Vance whispered.

"In Jesus' name," Austin, who just happened to be standing beside him ear hustling said before he hit Vance on the back.

"Dude, pray your own prayer."

"Heck, that's why I came by you, choir boy. I knew if anybody was giving the Lord His just due, it was you."

"And you know this," Vance balled up his fist and gave Austin pound, "Do you, AusMan, and I'll do me."

"Do you, V Baby, and I'll do me," Austin replied as their fist connected.

And as if on cue, the team started shouting, "Game time, game time, game time!"

Vance and Austin weren't the only ones on fire, because, by the end of the third quarter, USCC was leading the game by three touchdowns. Nothing was getting by Vance and every time the quarterback threw the ball to Austin, he scored. In the last two minutes, USCC's quarterback took the knee and the entire stadium lit up. USCC won the game.

# CHAPTER 12

Veronica tapped Kane on the arm and whispered, "I'm going to the bathroom. I'll be right back."

"You want me to go with you?" he asked.

"Nawl, it's right outside that entrance and you help Mom get on the field, and I'll meet you out there."

"Okay, be careful."

"I will, babe." Veronica leaned in and kissed Kane on the cheek.

Veronica moved quickly through the crowds of people who seemed to be doing a whole lot of cheering instead of walking. By the time she made it to the bathroom, there was a line waiting outside the door.

She got in line and looked attentively at the people passing by.

Veronica could have sworn she'd saw one of Vance's

old classmates, but as soon as she tried to focus again, the guy was gone. As the line moved, she tried to think of the guy's name. Then finally it hit her, *Davis something, uhm, but everyone called him D2.*

Veronica became puzzled. *I know he saw me. Why didn't he speak? And why would he be all the way in California? Maybe a group of guys from Florida came to watch Vance.* She shrugged her shoulders.

Veronica looked to the left and spotted another guy who looked like he was from her hometown. Although he wore shades, you could tell by his dreads and body build that it was Rufus's homeboy.

Veronica quickly moved into the bathroom. Call it intuition or a hunch, but Veronica knew exactly what it was. It was the Holy Spirit. Holy Spirit had not allowed her to lay her eyes on those guys for nothing. They were in California and it wasn't to see Vance play either. She felt it. All in her spirit.

Veronica had to pee so bad, she stepped into the stall and quickly pulled her pants down. After she finished, she washed her hands, took her phone out of the Bella Crossbody and prayed she had a signal. Thank God the new stadium was equipped with Wi-Fi in every space making cellphone usage easier. She dialed Kane. The phone rang three times, but he didn't answer.

If there was one thing her daddy taught her, it was how to hide in a crowd and how to check out her surroundings. There were four women in the bathroom who seemed to know one another well, fixing their hair and applying lipstick. And Veronica knew she'd found her cover.

# CHAPTER 13

Just as Veronica went through the entrance, Kane looked at J.J. It was like a keen sense or something, but they'd been able to do it all their lives. It's like they could read one another's mind, and right now, Kane's mind was telling him to go behind Veronica.

J.J. kissed Jade and told her he was running up to the restroom with Kane.

Just as they got through the doors, Kane spotted Veronica going into the restroom.

There were people everywhere, so he and J.J. stood right by the concession stand which was right across from the restroom. Kane's eyes were scoping the area and J.J.'s were doing the same thing.

"I wonder what's taking her so long," Kane asked J.J.

"Dude, you know women. She's probably fixing her hair and putting on some more lipstick."

"Man, Veronica is so not girly. She dresses like a fashion model, but the girl hates makeup. To be honest, she doesn't even need it."

"She is beautiful. I have to give you that, but not more beautiful than my Jade."

"Boy, sit down somewhere."

"I would be if you hadn't deactivated my brother switch."

"Man, I promise the Holy Spirit nudged me as soon as she went through those doors over there. I knew I needed to come with her. Why? I haven't the faintest idea."

"Mom always said, "Don't call Him something, when you know exactly who He is."

"Amen. And if Vee is not out of there in two minutes, I'm going in.

❧

VERONICA MOVED to the sink to wash her hands. It was time to get her cover together and these girls were it.

"Hello, ladies, I need a favor. I'm trying to hide from someone and I need you to walk out of here around me until I have a clear shot back into the stadium."

"Sure we will," they answered in unison.

Just as the five of them came out of the bathroom, they moved quick, but not quick enough. Veronica felt her arm being pulled.

She quickly snatched her arm away, and when she looked, she realized it was Kane.

"Baby, I'm so glad to see you."

"Thanks, ladies, this is my protector."

The college girls snickered and one said, "Can he protect us too?"

Veronica shook her head, but Kane could tell something wasn't right.

"What's the matter, Vee? You seem nervous."

"I was standing in the line when I spotted two dudes from my hometown. One seemed to have hidden from me, and the other didn't realize I spotted him. Vance, I think Rufus sent them here."

"I know he's a foolish cop, but do you think he's a dirty cop too?"

"I don't put anything past him. When people get caught up in pride and pick up that narcissistic spirit, they want to win and will do whatever it takes for them to come out on top."

"You are so right about that," J.J. chimed in.

"Well, he's going to have to get up early enough to fool a Booth and I don't mean as in eye awakening either. His spirit is going to have to wake up, 'cause no spirit can outdo the Holy Spirit.

"Come on, Vee. Let's get down on this field and I'm going to make a few calls."

J.J. and Kane walked behind Veronica but close enough to protect her. When they made it back to their other family, the team was just receiving their championship caps, and the trophy was being presented by the football association.

Kane called in a few favors and had two bodyguards at the gates waiting for them and two at the hangar overlooking the airplane. As he studied Veronica, he could feel that she was still uneasy. He walked up to her and whispered in her ear, "Vee, do you trust me to take care of you."

"Yes, Kane, but most of all, I trust God to take care of us."

"That's all we need, baby. Now, I want you to forget what you saw and celebrate this moment with your brother. He's so happy and he played his rear end off today."

"That he did. I couldn't believe how strong he looked out there. And not to mention how many times they called Vance Kimbrel. My dad would be so proud of him."

"He is proud, Vee. And of both of you. You are changing our town, building by building, and I'm so proud of you, too."

"Thanks, Kane. Look they are starting a video." Veronica turned her attention towards the coach and the jumbo screen.

"Our football team has worked so hard to make this win happen, and we'd like to thank you the fans of USCC for all of your support. This is a great group of guys right here. And I can't say enough about our seven seniors."

The crowd roared with cheer.

"You guys think that wins like this come from hard work on the field. But I beg to differ. These men are phenomenal in the field because they are good people. They have huge hearts and they aren't caught up in self-pride."

"Humble is the way," someone yelled.

"It sure is," Coach agreed. "It's the very reason I thought it befitting to take you back down memory lane. I wanted to show you all the wonderful things these guys are doing around the USCC campus and community. They're not only playing football, but they're also making things happen, and changing lives one play at a time."

◈

Vance, who was standing behind Jasmine, smiled as she turned to catch a tear cascading down his face. He was emotional. This was his last game for USCC. And although he was ready to go to the league, he would miss all the fabulous moments that came with being a collegiate athlete.

He looked over at Austin as the photo of them helping two elderly men came on the screen. Austin pointed and then yelled, "That's the day Mr. Murphy beat your butt."

Everyone who heard him laughed. They sighed when the next picture came up of Kane picking berries with a little old lady. Then the crowd laughed again at the next picture of her pinching his cheeks.

Vance's mind drifted to him and Austin's community service assignment. They were assigned to the Lakeview Nursing Home, an assignment neither of them had wanted. Vance would be the first to admit he thought it would be so lame hanging out with old men and women his grandparents' age. But instead, it had become the perfect hangout. He'd learned how to golf, play chest, bake cookies, treat a woman, read his Bible, and even how to truly love God. Much more than he'd ever imagined.

The only thing he didn't like was how hard it was to lose someone you'd grown to love. Most of the patients in Lakeview were well over their seventies and death was almost inevitable. Four whole years and Vance still had the hardest time letting go of those who died. Sometimes, he cried just as hard as the nurses, and his only comfort came from knowing they knew Jesus.

Even now, with them showing all the photos, he cried. And just when he thought things couldn't get worse, there was a picture of him in Kane's Louisiana crawfish t-shirt, being kissed by Elaina. Vance felt the skin on his neck crawl.

He quickly turned Jasmine around to face him. "Babe, I can explain."

And with one jerk, she snatched herself from his hands and said two words, "No need," and ran from the field towards the gates with Jade, Veronica, Kane, and J.J running behind.

Those two words stung his heart as if someone had just put two bullets through him. The entire family was now staring at him. Vance knew he needed to explain the picture to someone, but his mind was torn between following after Jasmine and hitting Elaina.

Vance walked over to his mother and Jessica, "Mom, I promise that girl set me up. I had an interview with her and before I knew it, she pulled me down into her with the towel around my neck. Mom, you know me. I would have never hurt Jasmine like this."

"I believe you, baby, but I also believe this is a mess that you have to handle."

"Vance, what did you do when she kissed you?" Uncle James asked.

"Mr. James, I swear I snatched away from her and then threw the towel on the ground. I went into the locker room and told Austin.

"He sure did, Mr. Booth," Austin who was now by his best friends' side admitted. "We even talked about how I would have hit her, but Vance just ain't that type of dude."

"We know he isn't and I believe you, Vance." Jasper Sr. patted Vance on the shoulder.

Vance fell into his mother's arms like a four-year-old child who had just lost his favorite toy. He was more angry at this moment than he'd been when he clocked Rufus at that hotel. He could have hit Elaina the same way, but even in anger, hitting a woman was never the answer.

CHAPTER 14

The caller waited patiently for the person he'd called to pick up the line. After the phone rang three times and he was just about to disconnect the call, he heard, "What's up?"

"Bossman, we were just about to get her. And those two brothers came out behind her. Then, after they were all on the field, we saw two big dudes and a couple more police than we'd seen all night."

"D2, I told you, she's not a fool. Did Veronica see you?"

"I'm not sure, but I do know she saw your homeboy Crawl. I could tell because I watched her looking at him as if she'd known him. He tried to dip after he realized she was watching him, but it was too late."

"I can't stand incompetence. I knew I should have handled this myself. Did Crawl go up to her?"

"Nawl. He just disappeared. Bossman, you know we'll get her. Sooner or later we will get her."

"Get y'all dusty tails here asap, and tell Crawl, he owes me one."

The call ended.

SELENA STOOD by the door trying to hear what Rufus was saying about Veronica. *His sweet, fat girl Veronica.* She'd never eavesdropped on him, but she had to know what was going on.

At first, he'd bought her everything she wanted and gave her full access to all of his money. Now all of a sudden, he was being really mean and he'd taken everything out of their account except a measly three thousand dollars.

What was she going to do with that.

She couldn't even buy a purse and a pair of shoes with that. And, if he was broke, he should've never married her. Everyone in Dade knew that he was still in love with Veronica. The fact was he loved her when she was a fat girl but was too ashamed to admit it.

Selena heard him clearly ask if Crawl went up to her. *Is he trying to get Crawl to give Veronica something? He must be talking to Derrick Davis, that's the only person I can imagine him talking to like that and I think they call him D2.*

She tried to get closer to the door to hear better but thought she heard Rufus move. Selena quickly moved away from the door and went around the corner in case he opened it. But after a while, instead of him coming out of the door, she heard what seemed to be glass breaking.

She normally never went into his man cave, but if he was this mad about Veronica, she needed to know why and what was going on. By the time she approached the door, she heard him scream or say a cuss word.

৩৯৩

*You can never send a child to do a man's job. Those idiots have wasted my time and my money.*

Rufus threw the wineglass and it shattered against the wall. Five grand wasted and he still didn't have Veronica. Crawl, of all people, knew not to play with him or his money. Now he had to pay.

"You can't find good help nowhere these days. If they ain't getting high or stealing your product, they stupid as the folks who think there's a place called hell."

"What's going on, Rufus?"Selena asked as she pushed the door open and entered his man cave.

"Did I tell you to come in here, Selena? What have I told you about questioning me?" Rufus stood from the leather chair and walked towards Selena.

He caught her around the neck. "If you come in here without my permission again, I'll make you regret the day you were born. Do you understand me?"

As tears ran down Selena's cheeks, she tried to shake

her head but the grip on her neck was too strong. Her entire body shook, and when Rufus released her, she fell to the floor.

"Do you understand me?"

"Yes, Rufus," she whined through tears and a hurt throat.

"Now, get over there and clean up that glass and you have one more time to question me about anything, and your momma will be questioning me about where you are buried."

"Okay, Rufus," Selena cried as she watched him turn his back and walk out of his man cave. She picked up the pieces of broken glass. *What in the world have I gotten myself in?*

❦

SELENA PICKED up all the pieces of glass, one at a time blinded by her own tears. *Rufus could have killed me.* She rubbed her hand over her throbbing neck.

Now she was stuck in a mess she'd created herself. Jealous and envious of someone she should have been proud of and now she was reaping all the animosity she'd sown. After the glass was completely cleaned up, Selena opened the door and walked towards her bedroom.

All she wanted to do was take a hot bath, but apparently, her husband wanted more.

Rufus beckoned her to the bed and said, "You know what I want. Perform your wifely duties."

For the first time in their marriage, he treated her like a tramp off the streets.

CHAPTER 15

Jasmine felt like her heart was about to explode. As the rush of warm waterworks flowed from her eyes, she turned and ran because she refused to allow Vance to see her cry. Just as she turned, standing right where she could see the action was the devil herself, Elaina.

Jasmine's first mind said, *Rush her and put those paws on her.* Instead, she raced out of the stadium and through the parking lot until she reached Vance's car. Her hands shook so badly, until it took her what seemed forever to unlock the car door. When she finally got into the car, Jasmine bowed her head and wept.

*Jasmine pull yourself together,* she told herself as her two sisters pounded on the window for her to unlock the doors. Jasmine refused. She was going to get back home even if she had to drive herself, and tonight. Sure, she'd heard both Valerie and Jade calling her as she ran from the stadium and just as she ignored them then, she wanted to do the same now.

To Jasmine's surprise, both Veronica and Jade knew exactly what to do. One jumped in front of the car and the other behind it. Jasmine was mad, but she wasn't mad enough to kill the people she loved. After she beat the steering wheel, Jasmine finally unlocked the door.

Veronica opened the door and pulled Jasmine out of the driver's seat and into her arms.

"Jasmine, I know Vance, and I know for a fact that you've got to listen to him."

"I'm not, Vee. He was in my brother's shirt so I know it happened since I've been here. Vee, I'm done."

"Please don't say that, Jasmine. You have to give him a chance to explain himself. Please don't run like I did and end up away from the man you love for four whole years," Jade pleaded.

"Come here, lil sis," Kane pulled Jasmine into his arms. "I know that hurt you, but I also know you are a Booth. We always shake back because we know who to put our worries and cares on."

"That's right, baby girl. God knows everything and if you really want to know what happened, you'll calm down, say a prayer, and ask for strength and discernment." J.J. patted Jasmine's back as his older brother snuggled her.

"We all know that you're hurting right now, so, whatever decision you make, we are with you," Veronica spoke as she held Jasmine's hand.

"I want to go home," Jasmine cried.

"Home it is," Kane said.

As they consoled a balling Jasmine, J.J. looked up and saw the limo carrying his family coming up the parking lot towards them. "There's Mom and the rest of them. Why don't you get in the car with them, and Kane and I will drive to the apartment."

"Thanks, J.J."

During the ride to the apartments, Vance called Jasmine over thirty times. She had no desire at all to talk and kept forwarding his calls, and then eventually turned her phone off. She'd been dumb enough to go against her parents' will, and now she was drowning in pain.

Jasper Sr. pulled his daughter into his arms, and Jasmine cried even more.

No one said a word the entire hour and ten minute drive to the apartments. Jessica would look at Valerie and the two of them used unspoken words with their eyes. But they kept quiet and Jasmine appreciated them.

Once they arrived, all of them got out the Mercedes passenger limousine and followed Jasmine. She paused at the door trying to will her hands to stop shaking. And as if she gestured for help, Jasper Sr. took the keys from his daughter's hand and unlocked the door. Jasmine gave her dad a brief smile that never reached her eyes.

The intoxicating pain made it hard for her to even express her gratitude. Once everyone was in the apartment, she motioned for them to take a seat.

Jasmine went into the kitchen first and took out the

two storage buckets for her shoes stored in the storage closet. She took them to the back and returned to retrieve three suitcases. No one offered to help because she was moving quick. For a brief moment, she thought about grabbing nothing but her important personal items: her makeup, electric toothbrush, water floss machine, and her shoes.

But the thought of another woman in her clothes, especially Elaina, drove her to packing fast.

"Dad, will you come grab my shoes?" Jasmine yelled from the back. She was moving quick because she wanted to be gone by the time Vance came home. Usually, she'd kept his car and waited on him after—and especially since they'd won—it would take longer. Or at least she'd hoped long enough for her to pull a disappearing act.

"I sure will," Jasper announced heading towards the direction of his daughter's voice. "Where are you, Jasmine?"

"In here. In my room." She opened the door and allowed her dad to enter.

No one was as shocked as Jasper to find that Jasmine had her very own bedroom. And by the look on his face, Jasmine had read his mind.

"No, Dad, Vance and I have never slept in the same bed."

"Little Girl, was my face that obvious?"

"Yes, it was."

"Jasmine, I'm so sorry. I just didn't want my baby to

be hurt, but judging by what Vance is saying, you may want to..."

Jasmine interrupted him. "Dad, I really don't want to hear anything he has to say. He should have told me before I was humiliated and in front of thousands of people and my family. Did you hear the crowd when that picture came up? They all know the history between him and Elaina. They also know that we're engaged. Dad, nothing has ever hurt me like this."

"Come here." Jasper pulled his now crying baby back into his arms. "Sometimes love gives us the best experiences. Sometimes it's the best experienced emotion in the world. But sometimes it can give you the worst experiences. But you have to have faith in love. Can you remember when I cheated on your mother?"

Through sniffles she thought and then spoke, "I sort of remember only Mom and I sleeping in her bed at some point. But vaguely."

"Well, I almost lost everything and everyone who meant anything to me. I didn't go searching for a woman to cheat with. Heck, I loved your momma and we were happy. I just got an opportunity to sin, and I wasn't strong enough to resist the devil."

"From the looks of things, Vance wasn't either."

"How would you know if you won't talk to him? That's the one thing that helped me mend my family, Jasmine. Communication. There's always two sides to any story, but I believe in this case, it had more to do with animosity than opportunity."

"Dad, you can't save him."

"Actually, I don't want to because you may want to stay here," Jasper said, using his finger to point around the room.

"Really, Dad? I'm hurting and you're making jokes."

"Yes. But all jokes aside. Jasmine, people can be evil and do some things to make others lives crazy. You cannot erase an evil move by shutting down or running. You've got to face this head on like you do new clients. Afraid and shaking, but determined."

"If I could just trust these paws, Dad." Jasmine balled her fists and held them up, "I might would, but right now, all I want to do now is just lay hands. On Vance for not telling me, and on this girl for whatever role she played. And Daddy, I'm not talking about laying hands like the Apostles do."

Jasper let out a laugh so hard and pulled Jasmine into his arms. "One thing's for sure, you are your mother's daughter. That woman will use her paws, as you call them, and then get an understanding later. I was praying that you'd be more like your good ole Daddy."

"Well, I hate to disappoint you yet again, but in every way I'm like Mom. And with that being said, if Vance knows like we know, it's best we part ways. It's best you take your baby back to Louisiana and I leave him right here to handle his mess."

"Hey, you can never disappoint me, little girl, and especially not because you're like your Mother. I couldn't think of another woman on this earth I'd want you to be like. Now, do you have everything before I call these boys to come get your stuff?"

"Just like old times, huh? I'm the princess and they are my two servants."

"That's right and no matter how many wives they get, they better always treat you and your mother like the Queen and Princess of the Booth throne."

"Thanks, Dad. You know just how to lift my spirits."

"You're welcome, baby, but you are still going to have to talk to Vance."

"Okay, one day, but not today." For the first time, Jasmine laughed and Jasper held his girl, grateful for the moment.

# CHAPTER 16

Vance couldn't believe what had just happened. He watched as Jasmine tore out of there as if she was a running back. Austin was just as surprised as he was. And now that both of their families were gone, they could talk about the situation.

"Man, what the heck?"

"Vance, dude, you've got to calm down. That tramp is standing right up there watching this whole scene play out. You've got to chill out."

"Dude, I swear if that girl comes near me, I can't be responsible for what I'll do."

"Don't say it, Vance. Man, you've got more Holy Spirit in you than anyone I've known. Now is the time to prove God and see if He won't work this thing out for you."

Vance had to think. *Is Austin deliberately trying to taunt me. He'd be the first to catch these hands.*

As though Austin read his mind, he said, "Man, I'm

not throwing nothing in your face. Just telling you what I know you'd tell me. Trust God. Trust the process. That evil witch is going to get exactly what's due her. Now smile."

"At a time like this?"

"Yeah, man, you can't let that thot see you sweat. Dude, laugh, now."

And Vance started laughing.

Before long, Austin announced, Elaina is storming out the stadium.

The two friends gave one another dap and then turned their attention back to the reporters and crews awaiting interviews. Vance wanted to just leave but he'd worked too hard for this moment and to have it spoiled by the devil wouldn't be fair to God or even himself.

After the field interviews, he and the other seniors met in the media room. Usually, Elaina would stay and do interviews for the school's news channel, but tonight, she was M-I-A.

Yet again, God saved him from himself.

Vance had never hit a women in his life, but he wasn't sure tonight what he wouldn't do. All he knew was he was angrier than he'd ever been at a woman in his entire life. And the gut feeling telling him Jasmine was catching the plane back to Louisiana, was making him feel nauseous and sick.

At first, he was hoping they'd speed up the process, but after he started answering questions about the game, his anxiousness subsided. And by the time the interview was over, he didn't even desire to face the music.

Thirty-five times he'd dialed her number, and she never answered the phone once. All the way back to the campus he'd gotten no answer. How could his Jasmine write off all they had behind a kiss? Then again, what if it had been him? What if he'd seen her kissing someone with his jersey on?

Vance swiped his eyes.

*Men don't cry.*

"Whoever told that lie must've been cold-hearted and mean," Vance mumbled.

As tears threatened him again, Vance grabbed a couple of towels and went in their locker room to shower. The guys were celebrating too loud to hear his meltdown and most were trying to get home as fast as they could to celebrate in all the festivities.

When he finished, he had all the determination he needed to win Jasmine's heart again. He'd give her all the time she thought she needed, but when his spirit told him to move, he would.

Vance mumbled as he dressed again in the slacks and dress shirt he'd worn to pregame activities. "If God be for me, He's more than the world against me."

Then it hit him. If Jasmine left, she probably took his car home and he would definitely need a ride.

He gathered his stuff and hurried through the door where the once overbearing commotion and celebratory noise had weakened. Vance was just about panicked when he didn't see anyone he hung with. He was just about to call for an Uber when Austin bumped him.

"Dude, you know I wouldn't let your butt walk."

"Austin, man, you are a good friend."

"Yeah, yeah, yeah. You just remember that when we get in the league and I need some money."

"When have I ever denied you the use of my coins with a little interest attached?"

"See, that part right there. That's what I want you to remember. Since Austin waited on my heart-sick behind after Jasmine dumped me, I'm going to loan him coins interest-free."

Vance laughed. "You're seriously waiting on me to repeat that?"

"Heck yeah. Either that or call an Uber. But, you my boy, though."

"Til death do us apart," Vance laughed. "Okay here it goes...when I get in the league, I'll remember this moment and won't ever charge Austin D interest."

"Let's ride, Clyde, since Bonnie done up and left your tail."

"Now you got jokes?"

"And I just got started." Austin laughed hard as they walked out to his car.

"What's so funny?" They heard her voice and knew exactly who it was.

Both Vance and Austin looked at each other before they turned to see Elaina. Call it a sixth sense, but they both felt something in the pits of their stomach.

"Elaina, what are you doing?"

"Looks like I'm standing here pointing a gun at you. Wha't say ye, Austin?"

"I say—you out here about to throw everything you've worked four years in college for away and for what? A dude that doesn't want you?"

"Shut up. I needed Vance to hear me out, and I knew he wouldn't do it."

"Okay, here he is. Tell him what you want him to know but bruh, put that gun down."

"Austin, if I have to tell you to shut up one more time, a bullet is going to go right through you. Now, get your tail in the car and take us to Vance's house."

"No, let's go to Austin's house," Vance suggested.

"Not happening. I want to go right to the place where Ms. Lady is, and I hope she gets the drift when you tell her to get out of our place."

"Why there? You don't want her. It's me you want, Elaina."

"Vance, don't tell me what or who I want. Just do what I say do and this button right here," she opened her hand to show them some sort of device, "is extra measure to make sure that both of you get in this car, and drive me like little Ms. Daisy to where I tell you to or we'll all die."

Vance immediately looked at Austin.

Austin's first mind was challenged by a slight nod from Vance. He'd always thought about being in this position before, and swore he'd do something to keep from moving to another spot. Now, here he was letting Vance alter his decision, but truth be told, they both had so much to live for. So, without hesitation he did as she told him but also did something he never did. Prayed.

Austin started the car as Vance was told to get in the front passenger seat. She sat in the back with the gun pointed to Austin's head.

# CHAPTER 17

Valerie and Jessica went into the kitchen while Jasper and Jasmine packed her bedroom. Both kept absolutely quiet until they knew for a fact they were alone.

"Jessica, I'm not taking up for Vance but my son never lies to me. He said that girl pulled him into her after an interview, and I know for a fact this is the devil. God would not have pulled us into worship so deep unless something was going on."

"Valerie, I was thinking the same thing. It was so unusual. I said one thing, and you another, and before long we were al caught up in pure worship."

"Girl, I kept asking, saying at that game, 'Lord, keep us from dangers seen and unseen and whatever you do, protect the pilot, plane, and the passengers.'"

"I know, right. Sort of why I didn't have much of a reaction when I saw the video. I recognized the enemy."

"And did you see Kane when Veronica went to the bathroom. Jessica, I know my daughter, and something wasn't right when she came back."

"I know Kane and J.J., and when I saw Kane dialing numbers and talking away from us, I knew something was going on with them too."

"But the devil is a liar. As sure as my mother named me Valerie Consuela, I have a God I can call on in the time of need."

"Absolutely," Jessica said as she reached for and squeezed Valerie's hand.

"It never fails, Jessica. When things are going good and life is so happy, the devil always tries his hand."

"His job is to kill, steal, and destroy. He's focused. We're the ones lazy and off track. If we would commit to prayer like he commits to his job, we'll beat him every time."

"You are so right."

"Just like he's tried it with Jasmine and Vance, but it will not prevail. I'm going to allow Jasmine to get on that plane and let her own actions be the best lesson she'll ever get concerning marriage."

"And you do know you owe me no explanation. We are in this together and it's the best lesson for them both to learn. I just have a funny feeling about my baby and that crazy girl, Elaina. A girl who will do that, will do anything and I just want God to protect my Vance."

"He will. There's nothing too hard for God. Well, it sounds like they're ready. I hear James calling you."

"Come on, Jessica. Thanks for the talk."

"You're welcome, Val."

The Booth, Jackson, Kimbrel clan boarded the airplane once again but this time with an extra passenger, Jasmine. Everyone was exhausted by the time they were seated. The stewardess brought them all a delicious meal of grilled chicken, a mixed broccoli, cauliflower, and carrots side dish, with rice and a special teriyaki sauce.

Kane was extra glad that he'd made sure to add a couple of extra dishes to their number because he wasn't sure if the men would want extra.

The stewardess served each of them the drinks of their choice and then some hot wet towels to wash their hands after their meal. When everyone was served, Jasper Sr. said grace and they each ate in silence.

The stewardess cleared the table, hit a button that folded and pushed it under the sofa, as foot rests came from under the sofa that now looked more like a recliner bed. The four old heads laid there with the women in the middle, and everyone else took to their very own recliner.

So many unspoken words still floated around the plane, but no one even cared to tell what each of them were thinking.

Although, they'd left the plane in worship, they'd boarded it with unspoken pain. Kane, wondering whether Veronica was really in danger, and Jasmine, whether Vance would really betray her.

As J.J. and Jade escaped to the private area for two, and everyone else seemed blanketed and pillow ready for a nap. Jade began to sing softly,

This is the time and in this space,
When things just feel so out of place.
We need You, Lord. We know You care.
I've discovered this so real and so true,
That I can always depend on You.
We need You, Lord. We know You care.
So now, I feel so close to heaven.
And I know You're seated on the throne.
Though the angels bow down
And they cry holy Lord, I come, Oh I come.
I come to You just as I am
We're wounded, but we know You're there
I come to You, please hear me Lord
I come because I know You care.

J.J. SQUEEZED JADE'S HAND. It was nothing new for her to write a song in the midst of pain, but tonight it was more special. Why? Because it was not their pain. The pains of others had revealed Jade's heart to him once again.

By the time they made it home, J.J. and Jade took a silent Jasmine in their car to go home with them at Jasmine's request. And everyone else hugged and parted ways.

Valerie scooted into the front passenger seat of her

husband's Porsche. As he closed the door, she buckled her seatbelt. She couldn't put into words all the thoughts going through her mind, as feelings of nauseousness invaded her being.

She closed her eyes and said a prayer for her baby, but for some reason, it didn't make her feel any better.

As James got into the driver's seat and buckled his seatbelt, he looked at his wife who now had tears rolling down her cheeks.

"Listen, Valerie, I know it hurts you to know Vance is hurting, but he's a man, baby. This thing between him and Jasmine will work out. We just have to give it some time."

Instead of speaking, Valerie nodded.

Sure, Vance was a man, and he could very well handle his own business, but the fact still remained, he was her baby boy. The only son she had. And if Jasmine was leaving, she should have stayed. If only to assure him that he wasn't alone.

Valerie went into her purse to retrieve her phone which had no call from Vance.

Usually after a game, as soon as he walked into his home, his first act was to call his mother. Maybe he was celebrating with the team. Maybe Austin had taken him to get a couple of drinks or something. Maybe he was too ashamed to call.

Valerie did what any other mother in her shoes would have done. She dialed his number. If he was out or at a club, he'd have to tell her that with his own mouth. But, he didn't answer and the call went to his voicemail.

She dialed his number again, and again, and again, but still, no answer.

Her mother's intuition was telling her that something wasn't right.

"James, I know Vance, and you've been with me long enough to know his habits."

"Yes, Love. I know he calls you after every game but this was a championship game."

"James, he's had other championship games and the routine never changed. Vance always, always calls me after every game. Uhhum," Valerie said as she caught her head.

"What's the matter, Valerie," James put his hand on her leg.

"Babe, I just had this shooting pain hit me. It's the same pain I felt when Vance Sr. was shot. Something has happened to my baby, James. Take me to the airport."

"Let's go home, pack some bags, call Kane and Veronica and then we'll leave."

# CHAPTER 18

V ance unlocked his front door praying that Jasmine had left with their family. For the first time since they met, he didn't want to see her face. Not that he didn't love her, but he had an uncanny feeling that if Elaina could kill her, she would.

He didn't see any other car in the parking lot except his. And he walked as slow as he could to get to his place. One mind told him to just hit Elaina's arm, but she held the gun with so much confidence.

*How could I not see this happening to her? How could I have been so blind?*

As if she'd read his mind, Elaina shifted, then spoke, "Vance, stop looking at me as though I'm a basketcase and hurry up and open the door."

A feeling of relief poured through him when he opened the door and there were no signs of Jasmine and the entire place was dark.

"Where is she?" Elaina asked, interrupting his thoughts.

"After the stunt, you pulled, she's probably on her way back home."

"Oh so you're mocking me, Vance?"

"Elaina, why don't you just go home and we will pretend this never happened. You are a beautiful girl and you can get any guy you want."

"But I don't want any guy. I want you, Vance."

"Elaina. We've talked about this over and over and nothing is going to change other than, I might not be marrying Jasmine because of you."

"Oh, so now you're blaming me?"

"You are the one who showed a picture of you kissing me to thousands of people, including Jasmine."

"Oh, so it was just me kissing you, Vance? I knew you'd find a way to spin the entire situation."

*Pow. Pow.*

Vance fell to the floor and Austin screamed.

*Pow.*

The bullet hit Austin, but in the arm. He let off a yell and fell to the floor. *Play dead. Play dead.* Austin closed his eyes as he heard her moving in his direction. He held his breath and dropped his head to the side. As soon as he heard her walking away, Austin scooted his body close to the bottom of the sofa where he could see them.

Vance was still breathing but now Elaina knelt next to him.

Austin knew he had to take action.

He could hear Elaina speaking, "I never meant to hurt you. All I wanted was us to be together. But I know you hate me so I'd rather kill you and then no one can have you."

As she continued talking to Vance, Austin carefully retrieved his phone from his pocket. The pain in his arm caused him to flinch. *Lord, please don't let my boy die. Lord please. And please don't let me die.*

First, Austin wanted to text someone in case she really did kill them both. The first person that hit his mind was Coach Felton. He used his thumb to text as fast as he could.

*Coach Felton, Vance and I have both been shot. Elaina Mitchell did it. At Vance place. The girl is crazy.*

Then he turned the volume down on his phone, disabled the sounds, dialed 911, put the phone on speaker, and pushed it underneath the sofa as far over as he could.

Vance spoke slow, "Elaina, just let Austin go."

She pointed the gun at him, "What do you think I am, a fool? He's dead, so get your mind off him. You broke my virginity. You turned your back on me. You blamed me for sleeping with Tim but never asked me if he raped me. You just took his word and left me. Then you have the nerves to flaunt a woman in front of me."

Vance mumbled, "I forgive you, Elaina."

Elaina screamed, "Don't say that. You're always trying to be a good Christian, but you weren't so good when you were all up in me. Where were your Christian values then?"

"Elaina, I loved you. You were the first person I ever slept with and you knew that. I thought we were going to be married, so we made love."

"Oh so now it was lovemaking? If you loved me, you would have found out how I got with Tim. He raped me, Vance, then he told you that I wanted him. And that's why he's dead now."

"Dead?"

"Yes, I killed him and no one knows it. Then I set him on fire in his car. Everyone thinks he died in that car explosion, but he was already dead before the car went up in smoke."

"Elaina, please don't do this."

"Don't do what? Love you enough to leave you here struggling as you left me? Well, it's done and I'm wondering if I should just kill you."

# CHAPTER 19

Selena slid out of the bed when Rufus started snoring and went into the bathroom. The only way she knew to erase the filth of what just happened to her was to get in the bathtub. Selena sobbed as she fumbled with her phone and hit the Pandora app. She selected the Casey J. station and sat her phone in the specially made phone holder bolted to the back of the tub.

She'd never felt spiritual, but there was something so uplifting about Gospel music that caused her to tune in. Especially, when she was hurting.

Her mind drifted to the look in Rufus' eyes as he held her in the air by her throat. For the first time ever, his eyes seemed to have yielded a tunnel to his heart which showed, pure evil. Selena closed her eyes as if to erase the picture from her mind.

For the life of her, she couldn't stop the tears from

falling. As the song *"Cycles"* by Jonathan McReynolds flowed through her phone, it was all the confirmation she needed that she had jumped right back in the type of relationship she'd just left. "The sad thing is that it isn't all their fault." She mumbled.

For the first time in her life, she'd take ownership of her part. She'd admit she only married Rufus to hurt Veronica, the cousin who acted as though she didn't exist. Sure, it had been a rift long before then, but all through school she'd tried to be close to Veronica.

Instead, it was Veronica who allowed the fact that she was a big girl to keep them apart. *But I might have felt the same way if my cousin, who was a part of the family that disowned me, was a cheerleader, and fine. But look where that got me. Stuck in the place I called myself hurting you, but in the end, only hurt me.*

Selena stood from the bathtub and dried her body.

She peeked from the bathroom door to see if Rufus was still sprawled across her bed. Selena glances down at the time on her phone. Two-thirty-five EST should be twelve-thirty-five CST, entirely too late to call her mother or aunt, Valerie. She put on her clothes but made a mental note to call as soon as Rufus left for work.

Someone needed to know what he was planning, and she needed to be packing. This was nothing new for Selena. The only difference this time was the fact she married the creep, but he only had one time to put his hands on her. Sure, he'd given her some sorry crap while he was on top of her about being stressed, but stressed wasn't his only problem. And she wasn't a fool.

Just like she'd left her ex and played a vanishing act, she was about to perform the same thing with Rufus.

Last time, she left with nothing.

This time, she was taking as much as she could get in her car, and she wasn't going without enough money to keep her hidden.

*Slow down. Don't do it all in one day.*

The same voice she'd heard when she bailed out on the last relationship, was here guiding her now.

"Could this be You, God?" Selena whispered.

The elderly woman who lived next door to them was always singing and praising the man who she called Jesus. At first, it fascinated a young Selena, but by the time she was a teenager, it got on her nerves.

Mrs. Hall was always saying, "One day you're going to need the Man, Selena and He's going to show you who He really is."

Her reply had been set in stone. "Well, when He does, I hope I live to tell you and you live to listen."

Mrs. Hall usually never replied back, but if He got her out of this mess, she prayed she lived to tell Mrs. Hall what her Jesus had done for her.

*If you acknowledge me, I will direct your path.*

Selena whispered, "I don't know what to say to You other than call You the name Mrs. Hall called You, Jesus."

*It's My name and My name will save you from the darkness.*

Rufus moved.

Selena stepped back into the bathroom, closed, and then locked the door. She fell down on her knees, with her elbows propped on the toilet. There was a time she wouldn't be caught dead touching a toilet, but right now, she felt as dirty as the toilet that held her upper body up.

She whispered, "Jesus, please save me from this mess of a marriage. I am so tired of going through cycles in my life. If You are the door that grants me my escape, tonight, I chose You. I make a vow to get my life together. I know Mrs. Hall said, 'It is better not to make a vow than to make a vow and turn from it.' But tonight, I make a vow, but with Your help to always chose You. In Your name I pray. Amen."

Selena had never prayed before in her life, but from this moment on, and judging by the empowerment she felt in her heart, it would be something she chose to do daily.

*Ship some of your things to your mother's. And some to your brother's. Only keep a month's supply in your car. Drive to New Orleans and, Selena, take the black bag in the back of Rufus' closet with you, in three days. Tomorrow, write all the numbers from your phone in your notebook and when you leave, leave the phone.*

Selena had no doubt that it was the voice of the Lord and directives from heaven above. She praised the Lord, saying what she'd heard Mrs. Hall say, "Thank You, Jesus." Then she slowly opened the bathroom door.

Rufus was still asleep and snoring loud.

She eased out of the bedroom door and went into the extra bedroom where she housed her belongings. She began to follow the instructions. Selena packed her two large suitcases with a month's worth of clothing: underwear, socks, shoes, bags, dresses, and jeans. Then she packed the medium suitcase with her jewelry, makeup, toiletries, and all the other shoes that wouldn't fit in the two larger bags.

She pushed all three bags deep under the king-size bed and made sure the bedspread was hanging to the floor to prevent Rufus from noticing her bags. He usually kept the door closed because he hated to see her junk, but tonight, she'd left it opened and it would remain open unless he closed it.

Selena glanced back at the time on her phone which now read 4:15. She quickly pulled off her robe and went back into the master bedroom. Rufus normally woke up around five o'clock by the sound of his alarm, and she wanted to be in a deep sleep by the time he woke up.

She pulled the covers back and eased into the bed next to him without making a sound. The blessing was he was a hard sleeper, and the miracle, he didn't even get up to go to the restroom tonight.

When she closed her eyes, with her mind she said, *Thank You, Jesus*, smiled, and dozed off to sleep.

"Selena, wake up."

"Huh?" She answered groggily.

"I'm leaving five-thousand on the dresser so you can buy yourself something special. I'm sorry about last night, Baby. Do you forgive me?"

"Yes, Rufus," she lied.

"I won't be home until late, so don't bother cooking. Order you something from that Chinese place you like, and I'll call you when I'm heading home."

"Okay."

"Go back to sleep, sleepyhead."

"Alright."

As soon as Selena heard the garage door shut, she got out of bed and quickly went to check the alarm system. She shook her head then thanked the Lord, knowing only He had made Rufus forget to turn on the alarm. Now, she could move freely without the fear of him watching her.

# CHAPTER 20

Vance tried with all his might to keep his eyes open, but he couldn't. He was going under and the last thing he saw was the gun still dangling from Elaina's hand. He could hear his name being called, but he couldn't will his eyes to open. He drifted and drifted, and drifted until everything was white.

VERONICA HELD the phone as Uncle James explained what her mother felt. "She immediately wanted to talk to you."

"Hey, baby, I'm going to check on your brother."

"Mom, do you think he's alright?"

"Nena no estoy segura." (Baby girl I'm not sure.)

Veronica began to cry harder. This was serious and something was going on with Vance. There weren't many times in her life that her mother just was not sure. And her uncertainties caused Veronica's heart to crumble.

Kane took the phone from Veronica's hands, wrapped her in his arms, and put the phone on speaker.

"Momma Val, Vee and I will come to get you and Unc in a few. Just give us both time to pack a bag."

"Gracias mi hijo." (Thank you my son.)

"Tu mamá de Bienvenida (You're welcome, Mom)," Kane replied and then hung up the phone.

He turned his full attention to the woman still weeping in his arms.

"Baby, listen, you can't cry as if you have no hope. No matter what your brother is facing, by faith, he's going to be alright. And you have to believe that God has him."

"I do," she said in between huge sniffles.

"Okay, so let's do this." Kane dried her eyes and nose with the shirt he'd just pulled off and caught both her hands in his. "Father, we don't know what's going on with Vance, but we know that You know. We ask You to save him, cover him, protect him, and most of all keep him. Protect us as we journey to be with him and strengthen his mother and his sister, in Jesus' name."

After Veronica calmed down and went to her apartment to pack a bag, Kane began to set plans in motion. He immediately called Dr. Strong to request the use of his plane again. Then he called his parents to tell them as much as he could. After he spoke briefly with his parents, he dialed his sister's phone three times and each time his call was forwarded.

There was too much going on for him to become
upset by Jasmine's pettiness, but then again, it was
extremely early in the morning, and she could have very
well been asleep. He left her a message explaining what
was told to him, and decided to allow her to make her
own decision to come or not.

After he finished, he took one glance around his
apartment, gathered his bags and set his alarm.

Veronica, he was sure, was just as gifted as her
mother because as soon as he closed his door, she was
coming out of hers.

Kane grabbed her, pulled her close, and planted a firm
kiss on her cheeks. He took her bag and nodded, giving
her the opportunity to go before him. Once they made it
to the car, Kane opened her door to put her in the car.
Even as he locked her in, he evaluated their
surroundings.

He hadn't forgotten what took place in that stadium.
As a matter of fact, his mind had been consumed by
nothing else. Kane was going to protect Veronica, even if
protecting her cost him his very life. If he were not
willing to die for her, as Christ did for His church, he
would not have ever asked to marry her.

Kane put their bags in the trunk, looked around, and
then got into the car. He locked the doors and then
started the engine.

He could tell Veronica was still so unsettled in her
spirit. He took her hand and lifted it to his mouth and
kissed it.

"Baby, it is all going to be okay. God is going to protect you and your brother. You have to remember that no weapon formed against either of you shall prosper. You understand."

"I do, Kane."

"I try not to always be so preachy, but I have learned that when I don't know what to do. When I feel I have nowhere else to turn. When I cannot seem to find my way out. I can always run to Him and the cross. I can always lean on His Word, Babe."

"You're right, Kane." She shook her head.

Kane felt just as eerie as she did. He knew for a fact that the weapons would not prosper, but also knew the surroundings where they formed was not the sweetest of places. Nor were the feelings you felt as they formed, all good.

"Vee, one thing for sure, God never said we'd always feel good and the processes we face always be good, but He did say He would be with us always. Let's trust that He's with us and nothing we face can tear us apart from Him or each other."

"Amen," she said as she lifted his hand to her lips and returned his earlier gesture by kissing the back of his hand.

# CHAPTER 21

E laina called Vance's name, but he didn't move. She tried to check his pulse, but she was shaking too hard to feel anything.

*What have I done?*

She put the gun in her purse and looked around for Austin's keys. Just as she snatched the keys off the table and reached to twist the doorknob, the door flew open. Two policemen dressed in back gear grabbed Elaina and put her in handcuffs.

"We need a medic unit. Two down. One has a wound to the upper left shoulder and to the side. He's lost a lot of blood and the pulse is faint. The other, a shot to the upper arm."

Austin began to cry out, "Thank you, Jesus," and Elaina looked his way.

"I thought you were dead," she screamed.

"Yes, you did but God kept me so you could go down."

The officer snatched her by the arm and pushed her out the door as the paramedics rushed in and put Vance on one stretcher and Austin on the other.

Everything was happening so quick after what had seemingly gone on forever.

"Is he alive?" Austin asked, aiming from an answer from no one in particular but fearing the answer.

"Yes, son," Coach Felton, coming up beside the stretcher answered him. "Austin, you are the hero in this and if it had not been for your smart thinking, we may have never known what happened to you two."

"Coach, I'd never thought I'd say this in a million years, 'It was God.' I know because my mind stopped thinking about taking her down myself. Like, I started thinking things I've never thought about before."

"He's real, Austin and finally, you know it for yourself. I'm calling your parents now. You hang in there and I'll see you at the hospital."

"I've hung on this long, Coach. I guess it's safe to say I need to stick around to help Vance heal."

"Sounds like a plan to me. I'm just happy you boys are alive and that you'll live to tell this story over and over again."

"Me too, Coach. Me too."

# CHAPTER 22

Jasmine woke up and sat on the side of the bed. She stretched and howled at the same time. The tenseness in her body alone was enough to make her crawl deep back under the covers. She rarely went to sleep with her curly locks hanging, but the pain of everything that happened, coupled with the two Tylenol PMs made her forget about everything.

She went in the restroom, did her morning ritual, pulled her hair into a high ponytail, and slipped into a pair of jeans and a t-shirt. As she glared at herself in the mirror, she could see the pain in her eyes. Vance had become just as much a part of her as her family, and being without him even for one night was taking a complete toll on her.

When she came out of the bathroom, she saw her phone light go out. And again, someone was trying to call her and all she wanted to do was get her thoughts together, cry until she couldn't cry anymore, and then move on with her life.

Jasmine grabbed her phone, went into the kitchen, and poured herself a glass of water. As soon as she sat on the balcony, she scrolled through her phone to see who called her. There were the thirty-five calls from Vance, two from his mother, three from Veronica, five from Jade and J.J. a piece, eight from her mother, and what looked like hundreds of voicemails.

Jasmine looked at the time.

Then, she looked at the time from the calls she got from J.J. and Jade. They both seemed to have left the home that morning and then immediately started calling back. She only wished that everyone would leave her alone until she felt like talking about what happened.

*They are just too pushy.*

She sat her phone back on the table and picked up her glass of water. It almost sounded like she heard the garage door go up, but then it was quiet again. At least too quiet for any of her loud, pushy family to be there.

Jade closed her eyes as the pain in her heart began to knock on her mind. And as if on cue, tears began rolling down her cheeks and she almost felt like she was suffocating from a heartache.

"Jasmine."

The sound of her name startled her to the point she jumped and knocked over the water glass causing it to shatter against the balcony floor.

"Dad!"

"Baby, I didn't mean to scare you."

"You did. You should have announced yourself or either called me."

"Yeah, right. Like people haven't been trying to call you all morning."

"I just wasn't ready to talk yet."

"Baby, you can never shut out the people who love you. We just had this conversation, but that's not why I'm here."

"Why are you here?"

"Vance has been shot."

Jasmine stared at her father. Then she leaned her head to the side and as she tried to take in what was just said.

"Jasmine. Jasmine," Jasper called out to his daughter.

"Yes, Dad, but what did you just say?"

"Baby, Vance has been shot. The girl who kissed him kidnapped him and his best friend, Austin, and took them to Vance's apartment. Apparently, she was trying to get to you."

"Oh, Dad. Please tell me this is some sick joke to make me answer my phone and talk to Vance."

"I wish it was. We got a call from Valerie about an hour or so after we arrived saying she felt something was going wrong with Vance. He usually calls her after every game, even when she attends the games."

"He does. He said it's his way of telling her that he's safe and also thanking her for always being his number one fan."

"He didn't call her last night. So by the time we flew

back home, she was getting more and more worried. Uncle James called Kane and Veronica and they all flew back to California. By the time they landed, Coach Felton was calling telling Valerie that Vance had been shot."

"Oh, Dad, please tell me he's alive. Please."

"He is alive, baby girl, but he's lost a lot of blood. They were able to get blood from Veronica for his transfusion and they are all there waiting on him to wake up."

"Dad, I've been so stupid. I should have just answered at least one of his calls. What happened?"

"From what we gathered, the Elaina girl made them get in the car and told them to drive to you y'all's place. Well, Austin is the only one talking from what I gather, and he said she was coming to kill you. Jasmine, it wasn't you who hardened your heart. It was God. Baby, had you spoken with Vance or answered your phone, you may have been there, and we wouldn't be talking about this now."

"Dad, I have to get to him. I hope and pray he doesn't hate me."

"How can he hate my baby girl? But I'm sure hearing your voice will make him get better. Uncle James sent the airplane back to get us and everyone else is waiting at the hangar for me to bring you."

The ride back to the hangar was just as quiet as the last two rides had been. All Jasmine could think about was how silly she'd been. The only thing he'd asked her to do was just listen to him, but she wouldn't even do that.

How could she say she really loved him, but she wouldn't even listen to him? How could she be his wife when she wasn't even willing to communicate with him?

Sure, she was going to eventually let him have his say, but look how easy stuff could happen to rob you from ever having that chance.

"Jasmine, baby girl, you cannot blame yourself. Listen, all your lives, I have tried to tell you that nothing just happens. All things. Not some things. Not a few things. Not most things. But all things work together for good to those who love the Lord. Jasmine, you love the Lord and I know you do. So, this was for your good. I would bet you a million dollars that Vance was praying you'd left him. When that boy was bringing that devil to his house, he was probably pleading with the Father to let you be gone. At least, that's surely what I would have been doing."

"Knowing Vance, he was. Dad, his whole entire goal since I was there has been to protect me. So I couldn't imagine him not trying to do the same thing then."

"We never know what's going on in the mind of another person, and anyone who would set up an ambush as she did on that screen, is capable of anything. Vance probably felt deep down that something wasn't just right. So, he was being careful for nothing."

"He was and I will forever love him for it. At this point, Dad, I don't care how the kiss happened. All I care about is that he doesn't die, so I can be the one kissing him for the rest of our lives."

"That's my girl and look, if God wanted to take him, He could have. So let me play daddy advocates...let this be a lesson that you can never run from confrontations, good or bad. If you love this man, you're going to have to stick it out. You have to communicate."

"I understand, Dad."

"And one more thing. People always tell you that you become one when you get married. No one ever tells you that Paul said when you do get married, it will be full of trouble. Do you think the devil is going to let you two touch and agree without at least three or four hits? Heck nawl. He's trying to dethrone God's power in your hearts. Expect problems, but know God always solves them."

"Thanks, Dad. I love you."

"You are so welcome and I love you, Jasmine."

# CHAPTER 23

Selena packed her three suitcases, all the extra shoes and purses she could put in her trunk and put the two boxes with clothes she was told to mail to her Mom's and to her brother's. Vashti lived in Jacksonville Beach with her husband and her brother, Bandarees, lived in New York.

By the time she made it to the post office, she was worn out. But she had a job to do. Selena borrowed the office's only dolly and took her boxes in one by one. After she shipped them to their locations, she giggled. *Rufus will really be thrown off trying to track me down.*

As she drove back towards their home, another idea fell straight from heaven into her mind. She picked up the phone and dialed Andrea's number. Andrea hated Rufus and if anyone would help her, she would.

"Andrea, I'm leaving Rufus and I need a get-away-car. Will you trade cars with me for a while?"

"Girl, I have one better. You know the new dude I'm with buys and sales cars. Well, we can get you a nice fast car and I'll have him to register the car in his business name. That way, Rufus won't know what you're driving and he'll never think you came to me."

"Of course, since he's all but forbidden me to even talk to you. Thank you for understanding."

"Girl, I'm always in your corner and you know I hate dirty cops. My dad's been trying to take that dude down for six years now, but he keeps getting away. One day, his stuff is going to stink so bad until he'll get exactly what he deserves."

"I think he's messed with the wrong one this time. I'm not the little money hungry golddigger he met and married. I know without a shadow of a doubt that I'm God's daughter and you cannot do me any way you desire and think it's okay because—in your book—I deserved it."

"Amen to that. I told my daddy he'll mess up with you one day and when he did, he was going to see a strength he's never seen before."

"You told him right. Tell me this, how long will it take you to get the car and take it to Public's groceries?"

"I can handle it within the hour. So, why don't you meet me there around two o'clock? By then, Rufus will be on duty across town at that school and we can put the stuff in your car in it. Then tomorrow, you leave your car in the lot and vanish."

"He'll think someone kidnapped me or something."

"Exactly, and I'm sure they'll have your picture all over the news so don't forget to wear a wig and get you some good sunglasses."

"Thank you, Andrea. You will never know how much this means to me."

"Yes, I will. Listen, whenever you put the hammer in the nail, make sure to include my father, Chief Andre Linnear. I'm sure Dad will appreciate you."

"I got you and you know I got him. It won't be long and I promise I'll never forget this."

"I love you, girl. Be safe."

"I will."

She went back to the house and used the things she had left to make the room seem as messy as usual. With Rufus being gone until late, it gave her time to follow each instruction. Selena bought an untraceable phone from one of the local hair stores. After she manually put all of the numbers she needed on the new phone, she hid it under her car seat.

When Rufus made it home, she was in full night gear and playing asleep. He kissed her on the forehead, and went to the bathroom when his phone rang.

Selena tiptoed to the door to listen.

*"Man, I'm still going to get her, but I heard her brother got shot. Everyone was talking about it at the station and sooner or later, she'll be news just like him. Yeah, I got all that in my black bag. It's enough to take me down and every bad cop in Dade County. Yeah, just what got Vance's life snatched from him. Who Selena? She's not dumb enough to go through my*

*stuff and after I choke the crap out of her, she knows not to play with me. Well, I better get off here."*

Selena hurried and got back in bed.

*"Lord, please don't let this idiot try anything with me and make him so sleepy that he goes to bed."*

She could hear him open the closet and then close it. Then he got his night clothing, took off his jewelry, and went back into the bathroom, closing the door behind him.

*"Now, Father, whatever You do, please let him forget to turn that alarm on again tomorrow."*

*"Selena, fear not, for I am with you; be not dismayed, for I am your God; I will strengthen you, I will help you, I will uphold you with my righteous right hand."*

Tomorrow was going to be a new day for her and whatever it brought, she was ready.

৩৩৩

As if God, Himself was orchestrating the plan, Rufus went straight to sleep and then woke up late. His alarm didn't go off and when he woke up, he left the house running. Just like the day before, Rufus forgot to turn on the alarm system. He also forgot to close or lock the safe where he keeps his service revolver at night.

As soon as Selena knew he was good and gone, she turned on the outside cameras so she could see anything or anyone coming to their house. First, she pulled the black bag from the closet, opened the kitchen door that led into the garage, and put the bag in her trunk.

She didn't have time to go through the bag, and she'd be long gone by the time Rufus would even look for her or come home. Selena went back inside and opened the safe. To her surprise, there was so much money in it she nearly cried. Stack by stack, she put the money in her huge leather duffle tote bag.

Selena was sure she had ten thousand for every finger he wrapped around her neck and another hundred thousand for every inch he held her off the floor by her neck. After she finished putting the money in the bag, she went to get some plastic gloves from the kitchen. There were two guns in the safe and because Rufus was as dirty as he was, she was sure those guns would connect him to something. Selena grabbed the two guns, the stack of bullets, and the pocket knife and put them in another leather tote bag.

She'd seen enough television shows to know that murderers always kept the guns they used somewhere in plain open view. And as sure as her first mind was telling her that these were dirty guns, it was also telling her that it was time to go.

Selena raced through the house and to her car. She threw the second bag in the car, let up the garage, and almost swallowed her tongue.

"What's up, Crawl?"

"Hey there, Selena. I was just about to ring the door-bell. Is Rufus gone already?"

"Yeah, and I have a doctor's appointment, so I can't talk."

"Okay."

"Crawl, go to the school on 9th Street. He's there until eight-thirty. But please don't tell him I told you that."

"I know, because he can be stupid."

"You said it and not me. Have a good day."

"You, too, Selena. Sorry for just popping up on you. Don't tell him I came to the house. You know how dude is."

"I sure do and I won't. Bye." She sped out the driveway using the button to close the garage. Selena wanted to be so far gone before Crawl even got back in his car.

She blew out a breath. "Thank You, Lord."

# CHAPTER 24

After the two-and-a-half-hour plane ride, Jasmine and her mother raced from the hangar to the waiting limousine. Grateful that Jessica could accompany her, but she secretly wished her dad would have come too. Jasmine understood he had a business to run. And with her being missing from the company for months, he'd become more active in the day to day proceedings.

Jasmine looked out the window almost not even wanting to engage in conversation with her mom. It wasn't Jessica. She was just not sure what she'd say and she didn't want to cry. As if Jessica heard her thoughts, she read her daily devotional and didn't say a word.

When they pulled up to the hospital, everything came flooding down. And again, as if she had a mother's wit, Jessica began to speak.

"Jasmine, God has you. Sometimes the greatest blessings come after we have lost something. You lost Vance for a day, now within the day, you learned some valuable lessons. People aren't promised to us, you have to communicate, problems are only processes, and God only knows what else He's been speaking to you."

"So much, Mom."

"I know. But get this, no one is judging your decision to leave Vance. As a matter of fact, we're all thankful you did. I could have been burying my child. My only biological daughter. But God! So, when we get out of this car, walk with your spirit high."

"Mom, thank you."

"You're welcome. Now let's go check on your man."

"Amen."

Kane walked out just as they were exiting the car. Anyone could tell he'd been asleep, but given their quick turnaround, that much was expected.

"Hey, beautiful ladies."

"Hey, sleepyhead. How's everything with Vance?"

"Mom, things are good. He's still in a partial coma. Doctors told Momma Valerie it's from the trauma of what happened and the loss of so much blood. Good thing though, Vee and Vance are the same blood type. She gave him blood and now she's resting."

"Kane, is he going to make it?" Jasmine asked and her brother pulled her into his arms.

"Lil girl, I'm so glad you weren't here and to answer your question, yes. The detectives told us that she came to kill you. Jasmine, it was God who hardened your heart so you'd get on that plane with us."

"Dad said the same thing, but it still doesn't stop me from feeling guilty. Like, I should have been there for him."

"I can half-way understand, but I'm entirely grateful that you weren't."

"I don't know what I would have done if the devil tried to take the life God created in my body."

"Right, Mom. And to think this girl was that heartless just does something to me," Kane replied.

"It's hard to put anything past anyone these days, and mental health is an issue. States all over this world have discontinued the help and funds to fund mental institutions and look at it even in our state. You call the police because someone mentally disturbed is off their medications or acting out. They take them to Louisiana Day, and the hospital releases them in two days. Now, what on earth is two days going to do for someone who's been off their medication for ten or even twenty days."

"Mom, you have a point." Kane nodded. "J.J. and I are actually working a case right now where mental health problems were a known issue, but the family did nothing."

"But the question becomes, what could they have done? Especially when the care of those with mental problems is now put on the shoulders of family members who aren't trained to deal with these issues."

"Well, if you asked me, some of it isn't mental. It's spiritual."

"Jasmine, as Jesus would say, 'By this, you have spoken correctly.'"

"Yeah, that's the truth. Just like the man Jesus saw in the graveyard. The Bible said he would even cut himself. But just like back then, the people in the town had left him in the graveyard to work it out by himself. Absent from us, not our problem."

"Son, you've said a mouthful. We are definitely turning into people who mind our business at the wrong times and for the wrong things. Think about it, if everyone would try to help these people, they'll have a better chance of living a more meaningful life. But, since it isn't in our family, we've committed to not worrying about it and that's not Christlike."

"Amen, so Mom, what do you think we can do as a family after this?"

"We can find a way to raise the awareness of mental health issues versus demonic actions. We can have a forum that will cause both medical practicers and preachers to come together. It has to be a place where people understand that all sicknesses can't be helped with medicine, and some things we think are spiritual are actually medical."

Jasmine wrapped her arms around Jessica's neck. "Mom, I'm so proud to call you *Mom*."

"I'm so proud to be the mother of three beautiful children and now, almost six."

"Well, let's see if Vance doesn't hate me."

"Girl, that brother loves you too much to hate you."

When the three of them made it to Vance's room, both Valerie and Veronica were rubbing his head and Uncle James was sitting in the corner reading.

"Hello, everyone," Jasmine said unsure of the response she'd get. But just like normal, both Valerie and Veronica left Vance's side to bring her a huge hug.

"We're so glad you made it. Maybe this guy will have a reason to wake up. He's in a coma and I'm so grateful to your Uncle James. He's been so helpful in getting us both familiar with the medical terminology."

"That's my Uncle James. Such an intelligent black man."

"Niece, that's why you've been getting all my money since you were able to talk."

"Uncle James, haven't you learned by now that girls know who to brown-nose?"

"Kane, don't be jealous. They know Uncle James is the bugger with the sugar."

"Oh goodness, there he goes with that," Jessica said and they all laughed.

Jasmine moved to the side of Vance's bed. She remembered that she needed to wash her hands and turned her back to everyone facing the sink. She especially needed the deterrence to keep her from weeping like a lost child. After she'd sang the happy birthday song two times, she turned off the faucet and dried her hands with the two paper towels she snatched from the dispenser.

When she turned around to face her family, Kane laughed.

"What's so funny, dude?"

"I see you still sing the happy birthday song while washing your hands."

"How did you know?"

"Because as soon as I got to the last *to you*, you turned off the faucet."

Both Valerie and Veronica looked lost.

"I taught them when they were young that they can never wash away all the germs until they sing the happy birthday song twice."

"Oh that was good, sister-in-love," James said and both Valerie and Veronica agreed.

# CHAPTER 25

Selena looked in her rearview mirror and didn't see Crawl anywhere in sight. She was glad that she wasn't in the house because her spirit told her that he wasn't just coming to pay Rufus a visit. The look in his eyes when she opened the garage was all the proof she needed to hurry up and get in her car and start the engine. If she had to, she would have mown him down with that car and then called the cops.

She made one necessary stop and then hurried to the parking lot where her new car awaited her.

As soon as she made it to the sweet black Mercedes, put on her wig and sunglasses, Selena heard, "move quick," so she obeyed. She quickly transferred the last of her belongings from her car which included emptying her glove box. Selena looked around to make sure she didn't see any familiar faces. Just as she got ready to pull out of the Public's parking lot, she spotted her husband's patrol car.

There was Rufus, leaned against his car, playing in the hair of what appeared to be a twenty-something year old. Selena quickly snapped a picture with her new cell phone and pulled off the lot before he noticed someone watching him.

"By the time he finishes playing with his toy, I'll be up 95 North and on my way to Highway 10." She giggled.

She couldn't believe she wasn't the least bit jealous. She just hoped that the young girl didn't get caught up with the devil as she'd done.

Just as she'd been told, she left her phone at the house and her car in between four cars on the lot. She'd also taken her license plate off the vehicle to make it harder for anyone to recognize her car and replaced it with the paper tag her friend's boyfriend gave her.

Selena dialed her mom and brother and put them on the line together.

"Selena, where are you? I've been so worried."

"Mom, and Bubby, the nickname she called her brother, I'm leaving Rufus. He choked me and I have a sick feeling he's trying to kidnap Veronica. Mom, I need you to call Aunt Valerie and tell her what I suspect and Bubby, I know he'll call you first to try to find me. Make sure he knows nothing. I left my old phone at the house, but I erased you guys numbers, but you know he's a cop so it won't take him long to find anything."

"We're not worried about him. I'll call Linnear and

tell him everything now. You know he'll know exactly what to do, and I don't want him blinded by the news you're missing."

"Yes. Andrea got me a new car and we tried to cover all the open spaces, but Rufus is a criminal and they have ways."

"Well, I'm surprised you knew to leave that phone behind."

"Bubby, I didn't but the Lord knew."

"The Lord. So you know Him now? I can distinctively remember when I got saved and I called you with the good news."

"I remember."

"Oh, so that energy mess is out the window where you should have left it from the start?"

"I'm not going to act like I'm all holy or something, but I promise He's been talking to me and giving me step by step guidance. At first, it sort of freaked me out. But then the voice was so calming, until I just felt compelled to obey Him."

"I, for one, and happy. Sis, I told you that the world would like to keep us in the dark concerning God because if the enemy has his way, he'll kill you, steal from you, and eventually destroy you. But just like the Lord prayed that Peter's faith would fail not, I've been praying for you faith to show up."

"Well, Bubby it has. I know it because, only faith, could have given me the courage to leave Rufus. Only faith."

"Praise the Lord?" Vashti yelled out.

"Mom, don't start. Give me a chance to build a relationship with Him before you go calling all your kinfolks and church-folks."

"I promise I won't tell a soul. I just want you safe, Mija (Mee-haw, daughter)."

"Mom, as long as the Lord is with me, I'll be alright. You just tell Chief Linnear that Rufus is dirty. Also, tell him that I put a package on his porch that I'm sure he'll find interesting. He just needs to hurry and get to the package before anyone else does."

"I'll call him right now and Mija, where are you going?"

"Mom, if I don't tell you, you won't be lying when Rufus asked where I am. Just know, I believe that where I'm going, someone will be there to help me."

"We love you, sis and I'm proud of you."

Selena wiped tears from her eyes. "Banadarees," she called Bubby by his given name, "I'm always proud to call you big brother. I love you, Bubby."

By now, both Bandarees and his mother were also crying.

"Bye, y'all. Please stop crying and whatever you do, please keep me in your prayers. I've learned my lesson and I don't ever want to repeat this cycle again."

"We will Mija."

And with that, Selena pushed the button to disconnect the call.

She turned up the radio and bobbed her head to the

music. She'd remembered to call her mom and brother after dialing *96 to restrict her number from appearing. This was how things had to be until she was long gone and far away from Dade County. And she'd definitely watched too many crime shows to know that Rufus could easily pick up the phone towers from the calls her mother and brother received.

Selena drove non-stop for eight hours and she finally stopped in Alabama to gas up again and to buy something to eat. It had to be adrenaline because she'd never driven this long without sleeping. She had only eight hours and twenty minutes left judging by her GPS before she was in her cousin's yard.

Selena got back on the highway. With the gospel music flowing through the car, she felt a serenity she'd never felt before. She thought about all the times she'd missed out on having friends or family because of Rufus. He'd basically secluded her in a world totally controlled by him.

"Exit left unto the bypass to Highway I-59 and stay in the far left lane to ," the GPS instructed her and Selena obeyed.

Once she was on Highway I-59, she decided to call Veronica.

By the third ring, she just knew the answering machine would come on but instead, she heard, "Hello, this is Veronica."

"Hello, Veronica. This is Selena."

"Selena who?"

"It's your cousin."

"Okay." Veronica paused, then asked, "What's going on?"

"Can you talk?"

"Yes, I'm at the hospital with my brother, but I can step out of the room," Veronica said, motioning for Kane to follow her and telling her mother who it was without saying a word. "Okay, to what do I owe this call?"

"First of all, I married Rufus."

"I heard."

"Well, he choked me a couple days ago and to be honest, he would have did much worse if he'd known I was eavesdropping on his call. Veronica, he's trying to kidnap you."

"Hold on. Let me put the phone on speaker so my fiancé can hear."

"He sent two of his goons to Vance's game to get you. He's obsessed with you, and he's so crooked. Vee, he almost killed me and the Lord told me to go. I obeyed and the only place I knew to come is to you."

"Okay, so what about your Moms?"

"I know that's the first place he'll look for me. He thinks I hate you, and he'll never think to find me in Louisiana."

"But, Selena, we're in California."

Kane interrupted, "That's okay, Babe. Selena, when we get off the phone, I'm going to text you the number to my brother and his wife, Jade. No, I'll text you the directions and you go straight there. No one will ever find you there, and we'll call J.J. and Jade."

"Thank you," both Selena and Veronica said it at the same time.

"We are family and I knew he was up to no good because I felt it."

"If Chief Linnear gets the bag I left on his porch, I know he'll be able to put Rufus away. Mom is calling him."

"So Aunt Vashti knows what's going on?"

"Yes, I couldn't let her and Bubby think I was missing. All the signs seem like someone kidnapped me and the last person he'll see on the home cameras is Crawl."

"That's who I saw in the game."

"Well, he was up to no good just as he's always been. Well, looks like I have only seven hours to go now judging by these directions. I surely thank you both."

"You're welcome and maybe finally we can be cousins."

"You don't have any idea how happy that makes me. I'm not perfect and I have a whole lot of goodness to do to wipe out all the bad I've done, but I'm trying."

"It's already been forgiven on the cross," Veronica said.

"Thank you cousin. One thing is for sure, Jesus had a whole lot on Him coming for me alone." She laughed and both Kane and Veronica joined in with laughter.

Kane cut in, "I promise, He had a heap of our mess on Him as well. But this I know, He stayed right there because He knew we would one day understand the power of His provisions. Drive careful and call us when you make it."

"I will. Thank you both."

"You're welcome," and they ended the call.

# CHAPTER 26

Rufus felt a sickening feeling in the pit of his stomach. He'd called Selena four times earlier after he'd finished with his hood rat and she never answered. It wasn't like Selena not to answer her phone, especially his calls. He'd made a mental note to swing by his house right after he did his school duty, but before he could leave the parking lot good, Chief called him to another assignment.

Between leaving the school and arriving at the scene of what looked to be a homicide, he called Selena four more times. "That chick's gonna make me choke her out again," he said and slammed the phone back to his side in the phone holder.

"Smith, what the heck Chief called me for?"

"Looks like this is one of your little neighborhood boys."

"Who?"

"Derrick Davis."

"What? D2?"

"Yep. Popped him like they were aiming to send a message."

"Let me check this out," Rufus said, moving towards the sheet covered body.

"Burns, what have you heard about this? This is your boy, right?"

"Yeah, he's one of the neighborhood dudes I know. But Chief, why you called me down here."

"Well, whoever killed your boy left a note for you. Here read it, but put these gloves on first," the chief handed Rufus some rubber latex gloves.

Rufus put on the gloves thinking whoever murdered D2 must have Selena.

"Look, Chief, I got to go find Selena."

"Selena? What's happened to Selena?"

"I've called her eight times and it's not like her not to answer me. Maybe whoever killed D2 done got my wife."

"I'm sending someone to your house now. You need to look at this note."

Rufus snatched the note from his boss.

*One down and Rufus Burns to go. Why y'all trying to figure out who killed this bum, find out why he was so tight with your boy in blue.*

"I don't know what this is about, Chief, but I got to find my wife." Rufus stood stoned-faced. Everything was caving in on him and at this point, he had no choice but to feel like Crawl was doing him in. He'd made the threat against him knowing that he too was just as much of a gangster, but he had the upper hand with the law in his pocket. Now Crawl was not only going around killing his boys, but he could also very well have his wife.

"Look, right now, you've got to do nothing but what I tell you to do."

Rufus furrowed his eyebrows looking deep at the man who was giving him what seemed to be a direct order. No one told Rufus Burns what to do and especially not in that tone. He'd been his own man for some time now. Things ran by his orders. He was the man.

"Look, I don't know what this is about. But what I do know is whoever wants to kill me probably went to my house. Selena is missing because she won't answer her phone, and I can't afford to allow her to get caught in the crossfires."

"I hear you, but as soon as I get ready, I'm going to drive you to your house myself. Now, who would want you dead along with this here young man?"

"Maybe someone I put in jail," Rufus huffed out before snatching the gloves off his hands and throwing them on the ground. He knew exactly who it was, but he was the one going to get him. Not the Dade County Police, not the FBI, or no one else except Rufus Burns.

"Listen, Burns, drive your car to the precinct and whenever I hear from the men at your house, I will call you. Go straight to the precinct."

"Yeah, yeah, yeah," Rufus said as he yelled back at the Chief. "If you think I'm going to the precinct, you're a

147

bigger fool than I thought you were. This dude is out here gunning for me and I'm going to show him that Rufus Burns is nobody's punk. Now, when I put a bullet in Crawl's head, then I will head over to the precinct and sit at my desk like the good little boy you want me to be." Rufus giggled as he put his legs in his car and looked back at the Chief who was still standing there watching him.

He had no choice but to handle this situation because he was the man on the streets. If Crawl made him look like a fool, every gangster in Dade County would feel like they could do whatever they wanted and he'd just lie down and rollover. Not him. He had never been a good boy, and he wasn't going to start now.

Life had already dealt him some hard enough blows and to let a two-bit hustler who wanted clout and street creds to outdo him, wasn't going to be how he would go out.

***

CHIEF LINNEAR LOOKED INTENTLY as Rufus walked to his car. All the information he was getting was almost enough to blow him away. He'd took up for the boy. Let him eat dinner with his family. Even allowed him to stay over at the death of Kimbrel. And to think he may have been involved was almost blowing his mind. But then again, his mother had told him before she died to trust no one but the God who always made the right choice: Jesus Christ.

By the mischievous smirk on Burns's face, he knew that he was going to do anything but obey his order. Chief Linnear looked around at the men at the scene with him. *Lord, who has your heart and who can I trust.*

*"Not Smith."*

"Smith, tail him and stay far enough behind, so he won't know you're tailing him."

"You got it, Chief."

As soon as Burns and Smith were gone, Chief called over two more of his officers.

"Garcias and Raymond, come here."

"Yes, Chief," they answered in unison.

"I know those two are just like Frick and Frack, but when I take one down, I want to take Burns entire operation down. I already know Burns is going straight to his house and Smith isn't going to call and say anything. When I know he's good and there, I'm going to call Smith back to the office and have them jump out squad there to get Burns.

"You two go to the precinct and as soon as Smith pulls up, arrest him. There's two more who I've been watching and I'm more than a hundred percent sure they are dirty too. Blackshire and Gillum?"

"You hit the nail on the head, Chief. We've been watching them too."

"But it looks like we've finally got those scums, thanks to Selena Burns."

RUFUS DID JUST what his boss knew he'd do. He raced into his house and went straight to Selena's room. There were no signs of struggle, but some of her stuff was gone. Rufus raced to his camera to see who was at his home and when he pushed rewind and saw Crawl, he was livid.

He went to his room to open his safe, and both of his guns and his money were gone.

Then he quickly jumped over his bed and went to his closet to retrieve his black bag. "Please don't be gone!" Rufus yelled as he opened the closet. And just as he'd felt that sick feeling in his stomach earlier, it reemerged when he noticed his black bag was gone.

Before he could swear, boys in black were everywhere. They cuffed him, and threw him in the wagon.

# CHAPTER 27

J ade put on a pot of tea and pulled some enchiladas out of the freezer. She loved Mexican food, but especially the kind her Louisiana mother-in-love made. Jessica called it Mexican soul and that was just fine with Jade as long as she had left-overs to freeze for later.

J.J. called her to tell of the news about Veronica's cousin who was now on her way to their house. From what Veronica shared, instead of Selena being a sister-like cousin, she was more like one of the characters on Mean Girls. But judging by what J.J. said when he called, the mean girl was now in need of the one she once hurt.

Jade washed her hands and put the food in an aluminum pan. Anything to keep her from doing dishes was a perfect creation. As soon as she stuck the pan in the oven, the doorbell rang.

She took off her kitchen oven mitt, laid it on the

corner of the cabinet, and sprinted to the door. She peeked at the overhead camera. *Wow she's as beautiful as Vee.*

"Just a minute," Jade yelled as she ran her fingers over the alarm key-pad making sure to get the design just right. Immediately the locks clicked. "Come on in."

"Thanks for having me. I'm Selena," the woman stuck her hand out in front of Jade.

"Girl, I don't know where you're going with that hand stuff. We hug in Louisiana." Jade pulled Selena in with a hug that immediately caused Selena to cry. "I'm so sorry. Did I do something wrong?"

"You've actually given me exactly what I've needed for sixteen hours. I have just been so full of emotions."

"Well, this is a cry-free zone. Cry as much as you need, honey. Come on, let's sit in the living room. My husband will go get your belongings when he gets home."

"Thank you, Jade. That is your name, right?"

"You got it. So how was your ride?"

"Long, but I'm just so glad to be away from Rufus."

"I'm not going to make you go into details, at least until J.J. arrives. So for now, let me take you upstairs to your room, and I left a brand new pair of pajamas on your bed with everything you need. We keep new everything around this house because we never know when someone is coming. Then once you've finished, press 211 on the intercom and I will come to get you and bring you to the kitchen. By then, J.J. should be here."

"Thank you so much, Jade."

"A cousin of Veronica is family to us. Follow me."

Just as Jade said, J.J. and Jasper Sr. were coming through the door as soon as she returned to the kitchen.

"Is she here?" J.J. asked leaning in and kissing his wife firmly on her lips.

"Yes, babe and how was your day? And hello, Dad."

"Hey, baby girl."

"It was good, wifey. But I promise things started going crazy as soon as Kane called to tell me about Selena. I put some things in motion and Chief Jones got in contact with Chief Linnear. Looks like Ms. Selena is a smart cookie, and she's left a windstorm in Dade County."

*Buzz.*

"I'm ready, Jade."

J.J. hit the button on the intercom. "She's headed your way."

"Babe, wash your hands and pull that pan out of the oven. I've already set the table and Dad, pull the salad and drinks out of the refrigerator."

"I. I. Captain."

When Jade and Selena made it to the kitchen, Jasper and J.J. rose from their seats.

"Selena, this is my husband, J.J., and my father-in-love, Jasper Sr."

And just like Jade, they both pulled Selena in for a hug.

"I hate that we're meeting on these circumstances, but I'm so grateful for you all."

"Any family of Vee's, is ours and your aunt Valerie is my sister now, so that makes you my niece." Jasper Sr. smiled and led Selena to her seat.

"Let's eat and after dinner, you can tell us everything. And Selena, my dad has called his good friend Chief Jones to come by to help us piece your story together."

"That's alright. I just need Rufus to get everything he deserves."

"Well, no more talking let's pray so we can eat," Jade said as everyone grabbed hands. "Father, we thank You for this food You have blessed us with and the newest member of our family, Selena. Thank You for getting her here safely. Please allow this food to be nourishment to our bodies, in Jesus' name. Amen."

"Amen," everyone repeated in unison.

Selena didn't say much as they rambled on and on over food as they usually did. Although she didn't say too much, she laughed a lot. The Booth family had a way of making you laugh, even when you wanted to cry. After dinner, Selena helped Jade clean the kitchen and by that time, J.J. was letting Chief Jones in the house.

"I think I'd better get my bags and Rufus's bag."

"No. You give us the keys and we'll get your bags. I'm also going to put your car in the garage next to Jade's car."

"Thank you."

"Hello, Selena, right?"

"That's correct."

"I'm Chief Jones. We had a slight run-in with your

husband while he was here a couple of months back, but he knew I meant business when I told him to leave and never come back."

"Chief Jones, this would be the last place Rufus would look for me because he thinks Veronica and I hate each other."

"Good, but after another hour or so, he'll be in no shape to find anyone. Gleaning from what I've learned from Chief Linnear and Captain Price, they'll have him in custody soon."

"Praise the Lord. So the guns were dirty?"

"One of the guns was the weapon used to killed Veronica's father."

"Oh God."

"Yes, little lady you have helped solve your uncle's death and only God knows what else will be uncovered."

J.J. came back in, locked the doors, and placed Selena's bag on the floor and chair next to where she sat. She picked the black bag up and opened it on the sofa next to her.

"When I left, the Lord told me to take this bag. It belonged to Rufus and he kept it in the back of the closet," Selena began to pull things out one by one.

"Can I have your permission to examine what you have?"

"Yes, Sir. That's why I opened it."

Chief Jones, J.J., and Jasper began to look at the papers as Selena took them out of the bag.

"Look at this, J.J. Looks like Veronica's father had

land, money, and warehouses that no one knew about but Rufus. But how did his wife not know?"

"My uncle was a cop and his only desire was to rid Dade County of drugs and gangs. He left them with a lot of stuff when he died, but Aunt Valerie probably wasn't concerned about stuff. His death hit her hard. Their entire family."

"Well, she hired Kane and me to look into some things she didn't understand. And from the looks of this, you've brought us a goldmine."

Chief Jones grabbed a paper and after reading it, he quickly called Chief Linnear and ran down some pivotal information.

# CHAPTER 28

K ane stepped out of the room to answer his phone. It was late and if his instincts were correct, Selena was now with his father, brother, and Chief Jones and they had some good news.

"Talk to me, brother," he answered.

"Man, this is crazy. Veronica's father was murdered by Rufus. He set him up a man to take the fall for his death and the fool had the nerves to document it. As a matter of fact, he has an entire crew of officers working for him. They seize drugs and always help one another get so much of the drugs and the money before turning it in. He has all the records to the hits and scores they made and the pay log to how he distributes the money to the officers. Kane, that dude is ruthless. God only knows what else he's done. Well, you need to tell Aunt Valerie and Veronica, they need to get back here as soon as possible. But how's Vance?"

"He's still in a coma, but his eyes fluttered when he heard Jasmine's voice. So, I guess, Dad can fly here to be with Mom and Jasmine, and I'll fly back with Vee, Uncle James and Aunt Valerie. I'm not leaving them alone with this situation all in the air."

"Sounds like a plan to me. Dad is here now, so I'll let him know, but from the looks of things on our end, Chief Jones has already contacted Chief Linnear there in Dade and they are rounding up Burns and his crew. Selena is one smart cookie and can you believe before she left, she dropped off some guns that were in Rufus's safe to Chief Linnear's house. She was smart enough not to take them to the station. Man, she's also just as pretty as Vee."

"Good deal. But, bro, no one is as pretty as Vee. Not even Jade. But all jokes aside, she is Vee's cousin and I'm not surprised at how smart she is. Now, we just have to make sure that everyone is safe."

"You right, scrub, but after tonight, your boy Rufus will be making deals in jail with the rest of the boys he's been down with. Man, you wouldn't believe all the information this dude put in logs. He had a legit criminal business and I promise his bookkeeping skills run rings around ours."

"Why it just couldn't be big brother or something? But, anyway, criminals are smart. How many times do I have to tell you that drug dealers are some of the smartest businessmen on earth? They just happened to get hooked up with the wrong products. Just think, this dude was trying to kidnap my baby. J.J., I would have blew Dade County up looking for Veronica and then your brother would be the criminal."

"Kane, you know we all are just one bad decision away from that title, but we would have found her. I just thank God that He didn't allow us to even have to experience that. I'm also glad that you followed the spirit and we followed her. You know, if everyone knew how wise Holy Spirit is, people all over the world would be obeying God."

"But you do know, that's too much like right," Jade interrupted and they all laughed.

"Brother, you all better get a move on it and we're gonna let Chief go home to his family. All the wheels should be turning in Dade by now and you need to get our family back home to Louisiana."

"Thanks for everything, lil brother," Kane said.

"You're most welcome." J.J. disconnected the call.

KANE COULD HARDLY BELIEVE ALL the stuff he heard, but then again, he could. He and Veronica had shared long talks about how her father had taken Rufus in like a son, but also how she felt Rufus halfway resented him. And knowing Veronica as he knew her, she was spot on when she felt something.

Kane walked back into the room and shared only a portion of the news he'd heard. Some things were best to be shared when they were on their own turf and especially not in front of Vance. Kane had always heard that people who were in comas said they could hear everything going on around them and Vance, had enough going on in his life than to be worried about anything else besides his recovery.

Kane was just about to become worried before Jasmine interrupted his thoughts.

"All of you go back. I'm a big girl and I'm going to stay right here until Vance gets up. Aunt Val, do you trust me to take care of him?"

"Jasmine, I know you'll take care of him. But until they have all the folks in custody, I'm hiring a private detective to stand at this door."

"I've already hired one and he's an old college friend of mine. His sons work for him and hospitals around the world use his firms when there's a situation," Uncle James said, and he rubbed Valerie's back.

"It is such a blessing to be married to a Booth man."

"Yes, it is," Jessica said.

"Okay, so it looks like we have a plan. Jas, are you sure you'll be okay by yourself?" Veronica said, patting Jasmine on the shoulder.

"I'm not by myself. I have the man of my dreams right here with me, and I'm sure he'll protect me even in his dreams. Now you guys go and please call me when you make it home."

"Okay, my baby. Momma loves you, Jasmine."

"And I love you, too, Mom. Now go before Dad and

J.J. try to go to Florida and do something crazy. You know you're the only one who will stop those two Jaspers." They all laughed.

"You are right about that," Kane agreed.

Everyone kissed Vance and Jasmine and said their goodbyes. Kane gave Jasmine some cash because he knew his sister lived by cards. He wanted her to be able to use the vending machines without using her credit card.

He also gave her all the numbers to the private detective's phone lines and the numbers to every doctor and nurse who had seen Vance.

Kane grabbed his sister by the hand, "Sis, are you sure you're going to be okay here?"

"Kane, I promise I wouldn't want to be anyplace else. I need to be the first person Vance sees whenever he wakes up and my only other alternative is to leave with you all and that's not happening. No one will ever pull me away from this man. I've left him once and almost lost him, that's not happening again."

"Well, sounds like you've made your choice, and I'm going to leave it right there."

"Please do, because it's the right choice for me. Kane, if Vance would have died, I would have died inside. I love that man over there with every ounce of my being and I told God, if He just let him live, I'm going to do whatever I need to do to help him get beyond this point."

"Sis, it sounds like you've really grown up on me."

"I have, but you'll always be my big brother, and I'll be your little sister and your sister-in-love."

"What a crazy family we have?"

"But I wouldn't change any of it for the world." Jasmine wrapped her arms around her brother and hugged him tightly. He kissed her on her cheek, patted Vance on the leg, and waved goodbye as he left the room.

JASMINE PULLED the recliner chair right up close to Vance's bed.

"Looks like we finally get to sleep together, and you won't even know it." She stood, kissed Vance on his lips, and sat back in the chair.

CHAPTER 29

Rufus put his head in his hands. His mind was running in all sorts of directions. Did Selena set him up? Was this her revenge for choking her? Was Crawl behind everything? Did he hurt Selena?

Although he never truly loved her, he never wanted her to die because of his mess.

"Where did I go wrong?" he mumbled.

*"What have you done? Your brother's blood cries out to me from the ground."*

"I'm so sorry. I'm so sorry." Rufus began to weep.

"Rufus, what are you sorry about?" Chief Linnear asked his once most promising officer.

"I'm sorry for so much." Rufus grabbed the tissue being handed to him.

"For the death of Vance Kimbrel Sr.?"

"Chief, off the record."

"I can't promise that, Burns."

163

"Please, I have to tell you, man. I know you knew how Kimbrel felt about me. I owe him this."

"Okay, off the record."

"I didn't try to kill him, Chief. I was a third year rookie and I fell into some stuff behind my cousins. They were all in a gang and I promised that just because I was a cop, I would never turn my back on my family. So, I get a call to come to the warehouse on NW 79th Street. When I get there, I see Kimbrel and he has three of my cousins jacked up. Chief, you know what Kimbrel meant to me, but you also know my family. He was just about to shoot my cousin who decided to run and so I shot Kimbrel. I didn't think he would die, Chief. I was going to explain to him why I did it, but he died on me. My cousin got a youngster in the gang to take the fall for the death. Without the gun, no one could ever connect me to the crime."

"Burns, but how do you live with yourself, knowing you took the life of your neighbor. A man who helped you get on the force and treated you as his son?"

"You try to do all you can for his family. I tried," Rufus said through sniffles. "I even tried to marry Veronica to care for her for the rest of her life. I know how wrong I was, but Chief the gang would have killed me."

"Off the record."

"Yeah, Chief."

"The old-heads always felt you did it, but I fought against it. I knew how close you were to Kimbrel and just couldn't imagine you'd take his life. I'm disappointed in you, Burns."

"I know, Chief, I know."

"All of our lives, from the time we are able to walk until the time we die is filled with choices. Sometimes, the choices we are stuck in between can seem like life or death. These choices can strangle the best part of you out and often make you live your life always reflecting on that moment. But here is the kicker, whatever choice you make, be it the right choice or the wrong choice, you have to live with the consequences of that choice. And Burns, that's not always easy either. Living with the fact that you made a wrong choice tends to set the tone for the rest of your life. When the devil knows he persuaded you into one bad choice, you become indebted to him your entire life. Why? He knows, he always has the guilt of that choice to hang over your head. Then when he has you exactly where he wants you, every other choice becomes connected to that bad choice. You continue to lie, steal, cheat, hide, do underhanded deals, become even more reckless, and all until you stand and confess that you made the wrong choice and the devil hates confession."

"Chief, I'm so sorry."

"I feel like you are, but I also know that you are going to try to fight with all your might to stay out of jail. The reality is, you are now right back where you started. You can either face the choice you made like a man and do the right thing, or you can try to find another way out.

DANYELLE SCROGGINS

But Burns, what you do from this point on will determine if you truly are sorry. Now, I have to read you your rights and book you for the murder of Chief Vance Kimbrel Sr. Like you, I could make the wrong choice and sweep this all under the rug, but what about the man who has been behind bars for ten years? What about the Kimbrel family? What hold would you have on me if I did that? See, the reality is, any choice that we make that goes with the moral standard of truth, becomes a lie and a lie never prevails. It only sucks you into creating more lies. Although my heart is hurting right now, I must make the choice to charge you in the death of Chief Kimbrel. I can only pray that after this, God will help your soul to find Him and peace of mind. Stand up."

"Chief, I have something else to say," Rufus said.

"Yes, Burns."

"Would you tell the Kimbrel family that I am so sorry and that I have always lived with the burden of my choice. Please tell Selena, thanks to her I'm finally free." And as soon as Chief Linnear stood from the table, Rufus pulled a gun from under his shirt and made another choice.

# CHAPTER 30

By the time their plane landed, J.J. called his family and gave the driver instructions to bring everyone to his home.

Valerie was reluctant because something in the pit of her stomach had warned her that she wouldn't like what was going on. As usual, she pushed for the sake of her children.

When they arrived, J.J. opened the door before they could even knock and led them all to the living room where the television was on CNN. They each took a seat.

"Just In," the news anchor said, "In Florida, Chief Linnear has just confirmed the death of Sergeant Rufus Burns. You may know Sergeant Burns's name for being attached to the family of slain former Chief Vance Kimbrel Sr.

"As of this moment, we do not have all of the details, but sources say that Chief Vance Kimbrel, Sr. was not killed by the young Sanchez Rubella, who has been serving a life sentence, but by Sergeant Rufus Burns."

A video of Chief Linnear was played. He said, "In a sting that has involved Sergeant Rufus Burns who shot and killed himself in our custody, we have arrested six other Dade County police officers on charges that stem from money laundering to drug dealing, and murder."

The news anchor returned. "We are awaiting a statement from Chief Linnear who is with the coroner, mayor of Dade County, and other officers and is about to take the podium. Let's listen in."

"At approximately nineteen-thirty, we took into custody our own Rufus Burns. Burns confessed to the murder of slain Chief Vance Kimbrel Sr. and then retrieved a thirty-eight Smith & Wesson handgun from underneath his shirt and shot himself. We are saddened by his choice to end his life. We have also taken into custody some other officers who were in an active drug and criminal activity ring with Burns as the ring leader. At this time, no names have been released until further investigations. We would like to respect the families who will all have to endure and get through this awful turn of events and would like to ask you the public to bear with us as we sort through all of the details in the upcoming weeks. There will be no questions at this time, but we will assure you that our team along with the Mayor's office, the internal police investigations teams, and the external investigating entities will give you more information as more is obtained. Goodnight."

"Well, there you have it. Looks like Sergeant Rufus Burns was taken into custody but was not searched as they would any other criminal because he was one of their very own. Sergeant Burns was questioned and made statements but proceeded to take his own life instead of facing the punishments that awaited him. We have already heard from the family of the young man Sanchez Rubella, who is said to now be traveling to pick him up after his immediate release."

"Lemmon hasn't he already served more than ten years for this."

"Smith, he surely has and we are sure that there will be some sore of restitution given to this family for the hardship that our police department has brought to this young man and his family."

"We will have more for you in the coming weeks concerning this case. Now to other news," the anchorman said.

"OH MY GOD. That poor young man. He kept saying over and over in court that he was sorry to his momma. And she was crying, "Tell them you didn't do this."

"I remember that, Mom. But he was in the gang and

they probably threatened to kill his entire family if he didn't take the rap for this."

"I hope he rots in hell for all the pain he's caused," Selena interjected.

"Come here, cousin. Don't say that. Listen, you have to forgive him. Not for Rufus but for yourself. If you don't, you will never be able to move on with your life. Do you see how many people you have blessed by coming forth?"

"Yes, my sweet niece. You have not only helped me and your cousins, but you have also blessed Sanchez Rubella and his family and not to mention all the people who those cops have hurt. You are a hero Selena and with God's help, you are going to get through this, but only if you make the choice to forgive."

"How can I forgive him? He only married me to hurt Veronica and then he almost killed me. He never loved me," Selena cried.

"Selena, mean and hurt people hurt people. The only way you'll ever be free of Rufus is to find freedom in Jesus. You said that you've found the Lord, lean on Him to help you to forgive. You just have to make the choice to forgive yourself and Rufus."

Selena blew her nose with the tissues Jade handed to her.

"We are your family now and we are going to help you get through this," Jade said as she took the soiled tissues from Selena and handed her some new tissue.

"Thank you, Jade. Aunt Valerie, I chose to forgive

myself for marrying Rufus knowing it was only to hurt Veronica, I chose to forgive Rufus for using me and hurting me, and I pray you, cousin Vee chose to forgive me for being the arrogant, jealous-hearted, and wicked person I was."

"I been forgave you, Selena, but I do forgive you again and again. I love you cousin and I'm so proud of you. Because of you, my dad can now rest in peace and I can finally move forward knowing that the past is behind me."

"Thank you, Veronica, and here is the only thing Rufus ever did that was kind. He left this for you," Selena said, handing Veronica a huge envelope.

Veronica slowly opened the envelope and pulled out first a handwritten letter. Kane laid his hand on her shoulder and she began to read.

*If you have this, I know that I'm dead, which I would expect won't be a sad thing to you because of all of the hurt I've caused you. But here are some things that I must say to you even from beyond the grave.*

*Veronica, you were the prettiest girl in the world to me but I could not bring myself to love you publicly because of how my family and friends made fun of me. Everyone was looking at your outside, but no one knew your inside like me. I only wished I could have been a better man. I only wished I had more confidence in the man I was but I was a coward. One looking for acceptance from a gang of people who should not have even mattered.*

*I took from you the one person who loved me uncondition-*

*ally and I know forgiving me is a lot to ask but I hope that one day you find it in your heart to do. You know my family. You know things that no one else knows. It was either I shoot your dad that day or they would kill all of us starting with you.*

*They knew I loved you and would do anything to protect you. I've lived my life always looking over my shoulder, doing dirty deals, trying to make the best of a bad situation, and all because I made the wrong choice. I did not want to believe the law I vowed and pledged my life to was strong enough to fight for us. To protect us. Now, I only wished I could have put my faith in it on that day and whisked you and your family away from Dade.*

*I do not want to believe that you will go on hating me, because you are too good of a person for that. Just know, I still had you on my mind. And I didn't marry Selena to make you jealous. I married Selena because she was the closest thing I had to you.*

*Selena is a lot like you and me.*

*She is so good through and through, but her lack of confidence in herself makes her a lot like me. Please, stay close to her and show her how to build confidence in herself like you did. She needs you and if I can repay her for any hurt I've caused her, it would be to make sure you hold her close.*

*Sincerely, Rufus Burns*

As both Veronica and Selena held each other and cried, the family gathered and around them and formed a circle of love.

# CHAPTER 31

Jasmine felt her hand move slightly. She slowly opened her eyes and looked right into Vance's beautiful brown eyes staring at her. She immediately jumped up.

"Vance, you're awake."

With a low voice, he mumbled, "Hey, beautiful."

"Hold on. Let me get the doctors," Jasmine said.

"No, I just want to talk to you," Vance spoke with all the strength he could have to make his words seem louder.

"Okay, baby, don't get excited. I'm here."

"Jasmine, I know you thought I kissed Elaina, but I promise I didn't. Baby, I'm so sorry. I promise to always tell you everything and never wait again. Please, tell me that you still want to be my wife."

"Vance. I know. I love you and I will forever be by your side."

"Now, you can go get the doctor. I'm hurting."

"Okay, baby." Jasmine put his hand down and picked up the call button.

"How may we help you," the nurse answered.

"Vance is awake and he's complaining of pain," Jasmine told the nurse.

"We will be there shortly."

After about three minutes, three doctors and two nurses walked in. Each assessed Vance as the nurse took notes. After what seemed to have taken forever, another nurse came down with a computer on a cart. After she noted Vance's blood pressure, she scanned his arm identification band and then took a syringe and explained before flushing his IV with saline. Then she explained that she was giving him a dose of morphine that would maybe put him back to sleep.

Vance looked at Jasmine. "I love you, Jasmine, and please don't leave."

"Vance, every time you wake up, I choose to be right here looking into your beautiful brown eyes."

"Girl, you know how to make the right choice, don't you?"

"I surely do," she said and kissed him on his lips as he drifted back to sleep.

# EPILOGUE

The entire family, along with Selena, was all back in California and standing around Vance's bed on Valentine's Day. So much had happened and both Valerie and Veronica couldn't wait to share the details with Vance.

Although, he'd been progressing quite well, they had all decided to break the news to him about Rufus when he was one hundred percent better. Even Jasmine agreed and made sure the television was never on the news or anywhere near news channels that might report the story.

As they stood around Vance's bed, he smiled at Jasmine who was dressed in a beautiful white laced sundress.

"Are you ready?" Vance asked his blushing bride-to-be.

"I've never been ready for anything more," Jasmine replied.

"Well, let's get this show on the road," Pastor Roderick Prince Strong said as he opened his small black book. "Marriage is honorable in the Lord and the Bible declares that a man who finds a wife, finds a good thing. So Vance, do you take Jasmine Shenay Booth to be your good thing. To love and to cherish her, forsaking all others, until death does you apart."

"I do, I will, I want to, I need to," Vance said.

"Okay, Vance, that's enough sucking up," J.J. said causing everyone to laugh.

"And Jasmine, do you take this man, Vance Kimbrel Jr., to be your lawfully wedded husband. To love and obey him, keeping yourself only to him as your earthly king, forsaking all others, until death does you apart."

"I do and I know it's the best choice I've ever made," Jasmine said.

"By the powers in me, I pronounce that you two are husband and wife. Vance, kiss your bride," Pastor Strong said.

And Vance slowly turned his body to face Jasmine in his hospital bed and kissed the love of his life.

"Yeah," Austin yelled, sitting in a wheelchair, then reached over and held out his hand to Selena.

"I'm Austin. I protected him and I think I want to protect you."

"I'm Selena, nice to meet you. And thanks for protecting my cousin."

"Austin," Vance yelled. "That's my blood and I will hurt you behind her."

"Dude, chill out. I'm going to be the one hurting behind her, so you take care of that little lady next to you and let me take care of cousin here. As a matter of fact, Pastor, is the wedding over?"

"It surely is, Austin. Vance has made himself the right choice."

"Well, I'm happy for him and on this here day of love, I'm going to make for myself the perfect choice. Ms. Selena, would you escort me to my room next door. I'd love to have your company."

"I will, Austin. I'll see you all later," Selena said to her family who was all laughing at Austin's crazy faces.

"Looks like love is always in the air around you people," Valerie said, pointing at the Booth and Jackson clan.

"It is and I'd have it no other way." Jessica said, shaking her head.

"Baby, I'm so honored to be your husband," Vance said, looking into Jasmine's eyes.

"And I'm so happy you made the right choice," Jasmine planted another kiss on her husband's lips.

**THE END**

# DEAR READER

If you enjoyed ***The Right Choice***, Book 1 of The Louisiana Love Series, try reading where it all started... A Louisiana Christmas Books 1 & 2: ***Love Me Again*** and ***Never Looking Back***. You can read them apart, but I promise you'll get the best of these families by reading those two books as well.

Please consider writing a book ***review*** on any platform where reviews are available. Book reviews are so pivotal in helping authors gain readership and so much more, and I would genuinely appreciate it.

It does not have to be long. You can write a few sentences to express or describe how you felt about this book and that would be awesome.

One more thing...

Would you please help me by recommending this book to your family members and friends? Also, recommend it to book clubs, your church members, ask your local library to get a copy, share it on your social media pages, and with your church libraries.

# PLEASE JOIN MY MAILING LIST

https://www.
danyellescroggins.com/danyellesmailinglist.html

PART I
BOOK 1: LOVE ME AGAIN

# LOVE ME AGAIN

## *The Funeral*

*Jade strolled up to her grandmother's casket, her hands folded and the only thing missing was the gold floral shaped ring with the birthstones of each of her children she wore daily. Like her grandmother, the ring had been a complete constant in Jade's life.*

*As the choir song a rendition of Ole Happy Day, Jade's eyes couldn't leave the casket. Her heart screamed, 'get up Momma. Please don't leave me. I can't live without you. I'm going to be so alone.' But her face was set in stone.*

*Jasper grabbed her hand occasionally, but she felt nothing. Then it was her time to do a tribute. Her heart willed her to abandon her, yes to say anything, but MiMi (the name she affectionately called her grandmother) was most proud when she was saying something in the church.*

*And although it was a funeral, it was still foremost and*

*forever the House of the Lord. So, like a zombie, she made her way to the microphone with one story in mind. With strength that only could come from the Most High God, Jade told the congregation of the day her MiMi told her she had, like her grandmother, done all she could do in the church. And the only thing she had longed to be was a deaconess. She said that when her pastor made her a deaconess, her job was then complete. And now, it was time for the mantle to be passed on to her granddaughter.*

*Then, Jade song a rendition of a song she would always sing for her grandmother. In spite of her not being a songstress, her grandmother had always made her feel like anything you do for the Lord was more than melodious to His ears. When Jade took her seat, her heart still filled with so much pain, she wondered who will ever love me again?*

*Who would do for me all that MiMi has ever done? Who will ever care about my welfare, hurts, desires, and dreams as she did? And for certain in Jade's heart, there was not one person left on earth that would. When the funeral was over, Jade stood by the gravesite still and stiff. If ever she wished to be the one covered by dirt, it was now.*

*Silently, she said good-bye, but in her heart she could never say good-bye. But she would say good-bye to everything and everyone else because there was no way she could talk herself into staying in the house or the town where MiMi had left her.*

*So, with all the strength she could muster, she kissed Jasper and promised to see him later. Yet in her heart, Jade knew that later would be far later than he'd thought. It was time for her to run, and never look back. Run, until she was too tired to run anymore. Run, until her heart stopped hurting and the tears stopped falling.*

## THE INVITATION

*Jasper Booth, you're invited to the Booker T. Washington Christmas in The Field.*

*This event will be one to remember for a lifetime. This ticket entitles you to bring one guest, and one guest only.*

*The chairpersons only ask two things of you: that you bring a generous donation for the Shriners Hospitals for Children Shreveport, and that each business brings twenty girl toys and twenty boy toys. You could also purchase products from Mr. Kevin, CEO of Playtime EDventures for the children's beds at Shriners. Your choice.*

*The Shriners Hospital has been a staple in our community since 1922. The wonderful staff has treated children from all walks of life, with so many different orthopedic conditions. Children are indeed our future and we would like to do something special not only for the children who visit Shriners this Christmas but also for their parents. These parents who leave their other children behind to care for an ill child, or who have the burdens of being off work without pay, or with very minimal finances, need our help.*

*Christmas is the season for miracles and blessings, right? And we, the B.T.W. Alumni desire to be the instrument that God uses to bring forth miracles and blessings to those who are in need.*

*Remember the dress attire is formal.*

*Please make sure to check the weather as we will be on the field and it does get a little chilly. There will be heated tents, lots of food, fun, and laughter. There will also be musical guests from our very own city singing Gospel, Blues, and Jazz.*

*We also will have a silent auction where you can bid on so many wonderful and extravagant items such as memorabilia, books, paintings, jerseys, and so much more, and all by local artists and athletes in the NFL and NBA from the state of Louisiana.*

*Some of Louisiana's finest have made pledges and donations that you will definitely enjoy.*

*Together, let's make this an event that the entire town will forever remember and most of all, let's do it for the children.*

*The Chairlady & Alumni of B.T.W.*

# CHAPTER 1

J ade sat on the porch of her grandmother's abandoned home staring at the leaves from the old pecan tree that covered the yard. Thankfully, someone had the good sense to keep the yard manicured. But you could still tell that the love once put into the flowers was gone.

No one had lived in the house since her grandmother passed four years ago. The uncertainty she felt in her heart at this moment caused tears to run down her cheeks. For some strange reason, the pain had presented itself once again.

The very pain she tried to escape. The place her heart persuaded her to abscond had beckoned her right back. She'd avoided what was before her long enough, and now she had no choice but face the facts. Her grandmother wanted her right here and this is where she belonged.

For four years, she was able to avoid all things family.

When the attorney called her the first year, she quickly sent the call to the voice message. Whatever he had to say to her would wait until her heart was able to receive it. The second and third time he'd called she answered but acted as though she was in an area that made it hard for her to hear him.

By the fourth time, his voicemail had all but indicated that this was his last attempt to reach her. He even made sure to declare that if she did not make contact, he would turn the estate over to the state of Louisiana.

There was no way she would allow everything her grandmother had worked so hard for to go to the state. The same state that had made turning the Oxford Street home into a business so hard that her grandmother had cried for many nights.

She did what any fighting granddaughter would do, she packed her bags, booked a flight, and mentally prepared herself to do what it had taken her four years to do.

As soon as her flight landed, she called for Uber driving service. She went straight to the Law offices of Jackson & Booth. Jasper Booth was the grandson of her grandmother's best friend, Leola. And her grandmother trusted Jasper with her life, literally. He had assisted her in making all of her burial and estate plans, and although Jade knew he'd only do what was absolutely necessary, she still hated the fact that it was Jasper.

The only guy she'd ever dated.

She sat ten minutes in the Uber car trying to will herself to go inside the office.

"Ma'am, your charges are going up," the driver interrupted her thoughts.

Which gave her two reasons to finally get out of the car—charges and up.

She slowly opened the door, got out of the car, asked the driver to wait, and walked towards the law office doors.

*This has to be done so you might as well put on your big girl panties.*

When she finally walked through the doors, the secretary greeted her.

"Well hello. How can I help you?"

"My name is Jade Bishop."

"So you are the infamous Jade? Ms. JB is what they call you around here."

"Yes, ma'am, I am. Is Jackson or Booth in?"

"Unfortunately, they're both out, but Booth left this envelope for you."

"Thank you." Jade reached for the envelope, put it under her arm as she adjusted the strap on her purse, and turned to leave the office.

"You're welcome."

Jade turned back and flashed a smile and said, "Have a good day," as she pulled the doors open and left.

*Thank you, Lord, for helping me to dodge that bullet.*

She got back into the Uber car and asked the driver to take her to 1500 Oxford Street.

Jade was certain she wasn't just afraid to face her grandmother speaking from beyond the grave. Four years had passed since she'd seen Jasper as well. When her grandmother died, so did her relationship with Jasper.

He was a constant reminder of the life she wanted to leave behind.

Jade paid the Uber driver, opened the door, swung her stilettoed feet onto the ground, and stood. She peered at the door as if it were an unfamiliar place. The Uber driver retrieved both her bags from the trunk and kindly placed them on the porch.

She thanked him and decided to give him a tip.

Jade sat on her grandmother's porch and three hours later, she was in the same space. She reminisced on her younger years. There were so many children in the neighborhood; all but two houses were visiting their grandparents. If she had her way, she would have never, ever, left her grandmother's house.

So many memories flooded her mind. Some sweet and others painful. But they were hers to have for the rest of her life. The Louisiana wind began to remind Jade that she was still on the porch. In fact, she had made no attempts to enter the house. How could she? How would she ever be able to do this alone?

The old wooden swing was as far as she could go. It still held the same beauty it did on the day it was built. And after all of these years, it proved to have more tenacity and strength than Jade.

*Girl, you need to get up and get in this house and take care of the inevitable.*

She kept telling herself it had to be done, but couldn't will her feet to do what her head knew she had to do. The later it got, the colder it got and allowing dark to catch her stuck on the porch was not a good idea.

Jade looked down at her Fitbit watch which now displayed 5:45. A whole three-and-a-half hours of swinging and thinking and still nothing.

No ideas beyond today, no thoughts of anything, just fear. Fear of the unknown that lay beyond the threshold of the front door. Would her grandmother's bed still be the way it was when the EMTs picked her up and placed her on the stretcher? Would her room still be filled with clothes she'd thrown all over the place?

Would she have all the stuffed animals Jasper had won at the local Louisiana State Fair since the time she was in the fifth grade? Would the house have the same welcoming feeling it always had when Jade was a child?

If the answer to her questions was yes, then maybe the fear of going into the house was all just a part of her mind. She was never scared when she was young, in spite of the fact the only thing dividing the house from the railroad tracks was a street.

But, that had never mattered.

The love in this house was so powerful it would have destroyed anything that was not like Christ.

Jade could feel a tear float down her face, and she quickly swiped her eyes with the back of her hand. How could MiMi—the name she affectionately called her grandmother—leave her? How did she know I was ready to face the world all by myself?

*"Jade, she knew that you knew Me,"* the voice spoke.

"Well, knowing You has not eased the pain from my heart or my mind. Okay, I don't want to argue with You. Can You please just give me the strength to go into the house?"

# PART II
# BOOK 2: NEVER LOOKING BACK

# CHAPTER 2

J ade dressed in a sexy cheetah print shirt and
brown leather skirt she bought from Jeauxbelle's, a
premium boutique in Louisiana, housing all things
sensual and sultry. Tonight she wanted to dazzle
Jasper Jr., whom she and others called J. J., without
causing him to have a heart attack.

Friday night's event had them all still in party mode,
and tonight they were celebrating Uncle James marrying
Veronica's mother, Valerie. Their quick decision to elope
went over everyones head. And although, they all had
questions, no one could combat Uncle James declaring it
doesn't take you two years to know when God has put
the perfect woman in your midst.

Then he argued that God never told Adam he had to
get to know Eve. He simply said, "I saw that you were
alone so I made you a helpmeet who is bone of your
bone, and flesh of your flesh," that also shut down any

197

arguments. The only thing to do was welcome Valerie into the family the Louisiana way—a party.

Jessica planned it and Jasper Sr. paid for it.

It didn't matter much at all that it was a Tuesday night, nor that most people worked during the week. To the folks in Louisiana, the week before Christmas and the week after, were just as much a holiday as Christmas itself. They were ready to party whenever someone said, "Come by my house."

After Jade's hair was laid—and makeup done exactly how she'd envisioned`—she was ready to enjoy the night. This was the first time in December, since her grandmother passed, that she was actually enjoying herself. Since the passing of MiMi, December was the month she spent at home crying about what she'd lost, but now she was praising for what she had.

Since Friday night's Christmas in The Field event, she and Jasper had been inseparable. Sure, it had only been a whole three days, but three days was to them a lifetime. Especially, after four years of being separated.

Their conversation that very night had given Jade so much clarity. Not to mention, moved her in a different financial bracket.

She now realized why her grandmother budgeted for everything. MiMi was trying to make sure Jade never wanted for money. She'd intellectually and strategically invested Jade's parents' burial insurance money to secure their child's future and she did it well.

With Jasper Jr. helping her, they'd amassed a fortune.

He'd started finding places for her to invest in when they were only freshmen in college. When those investments yielded great dividends, he found more places. And the end results was him owning one of the six lofts in the building he lived in, and at the end of her life, she secured his future with a sweet bag, too.

To know she was rich hadn't changed much.

Jade was a wise spender because she always had to be. The only thing different now was she could buy two bags of popcorn instead of one. She was still conservative and most of the time, acted like she was still scraping pennies together to make a dollar.

Jasper told her to splurge a little, but splurging was not in her DNA, whether she was rich or poor.

The only huge purchase she'd made was buying those Playtime EDventures sheets for the entire children's floor at Louisiana Day Hospital. She remembered telling God when she bought a couple of sets, that if she had money she'd do just like Jessica. Invest in Playtime EDventures by buying their products for an entire hospital.

Jade knew the Lord heard her and was holding her to just that. She believed wholeheartedly, He'd given her that money to live free from the burdens brought on by lack and to take care of her heart's desires, which included blessing others.

With this one splurge outfit, she was ready to step out on the town. She, Jasmine, and Veronica spent all day Monday trying to find outfits for tonight's party. It was totally easy for Jasmine because it involved spending money. For her, still a preposterous task. She finally relied upon Jasmine to talk her into what she thought was the perfect shirt and skirt, to match the pair of black boots she already owned.

But for some reason, she still felt a little too under-dressed.

Jade roamed the house patiently awaiting the sound of Jasper's engine. She was praying he came quick before she talked herself out of the sexy outfit. Only seconds later, she heard the doorbell ring. Because she didn't hear the roaring of his Porsche's engine, she thought maybe it was someone else.

She tugged on the leather skirt a little on the sides to smooth it and then asked, "Who is it?"

"Your earth-king."

Jade swung the door open and a stunned Jasper stood in silence.

Was it shock? Was he blown away? What?

She finally decided to say something. "Would you like to come in?"

"Wow!"

"Wow, you like or wow, I need to change?"

"Wow, I love, and no you don't have to change. But I can bet all types of money Jasmine found that top."

"You know your sister, huh?"

"That girl always loves stuff hanging off her shoulders. But promise me this, you'll only dress like this when you are with me."

"Are you sure you don't want me to change? I've learned that even in my dress, I want to represent God. I've also learned that you can look at a woman with a short skirt and feel whoremonger. But you can look across the room at another woman with the same skirt on and say, 'cute.'"

"Jade, it's not the clothes. I believe it's the spirit that resides in the one wearing the clothes."

"Okay, so I'm good?"

"Perfect. I'm comfortable and you're fine. I guess, I'm the typical man who wants no other man to even see your beauty. But Jade, that's impossible. As soon as you smile or even speak, people can't help but feel the glory in your life."

"Thanks, Jasper and we better hurry before we are really late."

"Okay, I will set the alarm and you start making your way to the car."

Jade stepped out onto the porch and before long, Jasper was beside her helping her down the stairs.

She draped her black shawl over her arm and carefully held tight to his hand. Jade loved her new boots, but the heels made her cautious. When she saw the black boots, prior to learning she had plenty of cash, she had to have them. They were eighty-five-percent off the original price, and she would have never paid the original price. The only thing...she wasn't sure if she'd be able to handle the heel.

When she was firmly on the ground she whispered,

"Thank you Lord." She couldn't imagine looking all sexy and Jasper having to pick her up off the ground.

The things a woman will do and wear to entice a man.

He opened his car's passenger door and allowed her to get in. Once she was in, he bent down and kissed her on the cheek.

"I love you, Jade."

"I love you, too, Jasper Jr."

It was nice hearing him say those words. She knew for a fact she didn't deserve him nor his love. Jade was so grateful God had given her another opportunity to be loved by him again. This time, she wouldn't take his love for granted. Neither would she allow the things she felt to interfere with the path God set.

# ABOUT THE AUTHOR

In addition to being an author, Danyelle Scroggins is the Pastor of New Vessels Ministries in Shreveport, Louisiana. She is the wife of Pastor Reynard Scroggins and the mother of three young adults: Raiyawna, Dobrielle, and Dwight Jr. by birth; and two: Reynard II and Gabriel by marriage. The privilege of being a mother graciously presented her with the impressive task of now being the grandmother of Emiya'rai Grace and RC III.

She has earned an Associate's Degree in Psychology, Bachelors in Interdisciplinary Studies in Psychology and Biblical Studies, and a Masters in Religious Education.

Danyelle loves writing, and you can discover more about her work, both fiction and nonfiction, by visiting Amazon and searching her name or by visiting her website.

She loves to hear from you, her readers! Feel free to contact Danyelle to book speaking engagements or learn more about her books via her website www. danyellescroggins.com.

# PUBLISHER'S NOTE

Divinely Sown Publishing Appreciates You!

We are grateful you have decided to read another Divinely Sown Publishing book. We are committed to bringing you books divinely sown into our hearts, keeping you, our readers, reading and sharing with others. We pray in every book you see God and come to know Him as your very own personal Savior.

We would love to hear from you! You can email us at divinelysownpublishing@gmail.com. Until your next book experience with us....Be Blessed!

Sincerely,
The Staff of Divinely Sown Publishing

# OTHER BOOKS BY DANYELLE SCROGGINS

TRY THE:

***E Love Series Books 1-5.***

**Enduring Love**

https://www. danyellescroggins.com/enduringlove.html

**Enchanting Love**

https://www. danyellescroggins.com/enchantinglove.html

**Everlasting Love**

https://www. danyellescroggins.com/everlastinglove.html

**Extraordinary Love**

https://www. danyellescroggins.com/extraordinarylove.html

**Extravagant Love**

https://www. danyellescroggins.com/extravagantlove.html

Made in the USA
Columbia, SC
26 September 2024

42437749R00133